Is simple, unaffected Timothy Lea too nice
for the hard world of film-making?
Will he be able to cope with smooth blue
film producer, Justin Tymely, and
outrageous director, Ken Loser? And
those girls: Sandra Virgin, Sadie Masoch,
Dawn Lovelost, Samantha Toots and the
rest of them. They all seem interested in
only one thing.
Even with Sidney's help will Timmy be
able to cope?
There's only one way to find out. . . .

Confessions of a
Film Extra

TIMOTHY LEA

SPHERE BOOKS LIMITED
30/32 Gray's Inn Road, London WC1X 8JL

First published in Great Britain
by Sphere Books Ltd 1973
Copyright © Christopher Wood 1973
Reprinted October 1973

TRADE
MARK

Set in Linotype Baskerville

Printed in Great Britain by
Hazell Watson & Viney Ltd
Aylesbury, Bucks

ISBN 0 7221 9320 3

CONTENTS

Chapter One

In which Timmy finds that nephew Jason has become a child tele personality and meets Miss Mealie, the star of the programme, with unfortunate consequences.

Chapter Two

In which Timmy gets much closer to Miss Mealie and receives a great surprise.

Chapter Three

In which Timmy meets dynamic impresario, Justin Tymely. Also voluptuous Sandra Virgin and her friendly doggy, with whom he becomes better acquainted.

Chapter Four

In which brother-in-law Sidney is introduced to the movie business and shares an interesting lunch-time experience with Timmy and Samantha and Sadie, two fun-loving filmic personalities.

Chapter Five

In which Timmy comes face to face with the controversial director, Ken Loser and attempts to rescue his excitable sister, Rosie, from an unsavoury entanglement with Glint Thrust, virile movie star.

Chapter Six

In which Timmy is taken to the bosom of actress Dawn Lovelost and a passionate lady extra, and becomes an actor. Also in which he visits the studio in the company of mum, dad and Sidney and receives another surprise.

Chapter Seven

In which Timmy attends a very unusual film première, dad disgraces himself, and Timmy renews a close acquaintanceship with an old friend in very embarrassing circumstances.

Chapter Eight

In which good fortune and cunning turn disaster into triumph and Timmy and Sid go to Cyprus to make another movie. They find that the organisation of this enterprise leaves something to be desired.

Chapter Nine

In which violence breaks out and Timmy takes shelter in a building full of ladies possessing talents very close to his heart.

Chapter Ten

In which Timmy's latest film is premièred with arresting consequences.

CHAPTER ONE

I do not fancy burning down the warehouse with Sidney, so when the train pulls in at Euston, I slide off home to spend a few days with mum and dad. Sidney takes it badly of course, but I am quite Adam Faith about it and will not be Budgied. I mean, I have been through it all too many times before. Whenever there is knavery to be done and Sid says 'we' he really means me. And with my luck the matches would be damp and I would try striking one on a copper's leg while Sid was keeping watch from the nearest boozer with his back to the window.

For those unfortunate enough to have found their local bookshops sold out of 'Confessions of a Travelling Salesman', I had better point out that my evil brother-in-law Sidney Noggett, needed to burn down a warehouse full of unusable empire-made, multi-purpose cleaners because it was his only means of recovering the money he had laid out in a disastrous deal with a very unworthy Japanese gentleman by the name of Mr. Ishowi.

Scraggs Lane, Clapham is the ancestral home of the Leas, although my mum always points out to people that we live at the Wandsworth Common end of it. She thinks it sounds more refined. A much nicer class of person gets mugged on Wandsworth Common.

When I get to the end of the road it is looking even scruffier than usual because they are pulling down one side of the street and a lot of people have taken the opportunity of dumping their rubbish along the pavement. It looks like a holiday camp for bluebottles. I am surprised that the slipstream from the ball and chain has not knocked down our house. Sidney always said that it was only kept upright by the woodworm joining together and holding hands.

Still, like the poet says, be it ever so tumbledown, there is no place like home, and I cannot help feeling sad as I watch the lousy old place falling apart. All these high-rise flats springing up like fast-growing mushrooms from a cowpat. Only the boozers left like fish heads to remind you of the rest of the body that has been gobbled up. Go in some of those pubs and they have to have the lights on all the time because there are so many blooming great buildings leaning on them, shutting out the light.

It is about five o'clock when I get home and I am not altogether surprised when dad opens the front door to me. He puts in time at the Lost Property Office and brings a lot of his work home with him. So much so that he is sometimes asked to take it back again. He is also convinced that atomic tests and fluoride in the water supply are sapping his natural juices and for that reason he is dead cautious about going to work unless he feels one hundred per cent. One hundred per cent what, I have never been able to discover. Suffice to say that there are usually one or two days a week when he is 'resting up for the big push' as he puts it. Why the Lost Property Office have not got the big push in first I will never know.

Dad's face when he sees me undergoes remarkably little change except that his mouth drops by one sixteenth of an inch.

'Oh,' he says, 'it's you. What disaster brings you home?'

'Your charm school closed down for the holidays, has it, dad?'

'Don't give me none of your lip. I know you don't come round here unless you want something.' Marvellous, isn't it? I have only just appeared on the doorstep and he is within an ace of going into his 'you use this place like a hotel' routine.

'I wanted to see you and mum,' I say patiently. 'This is my home, dad.'

'Only when things are getting too hot for you somewhere else.'

Trouble with the old bleeder is that he is usually right.

'Oh, dad,' I say reproachfully, 'dad.' I let my voice tail away like I am too choked and hurt for words, and give a

8

little misunderstood shake of the head. Believe me, Oscars have been won for far worse performances.

'Well, come in if you're coming,' says dad, singularly unmoved. 'Don't hang about there like a great Jessy.'

I cross the threshold and am greeted by the odour of boiled cabbage and rising damp that always spells out home – or, more appropriately, smells out home. The hall looks the same except for a large barometer hanging between the moose head and the tin hat and gas mask. Dad was an air-raid warden during the last war and does not like people to forget the fact. He and mum live in the past, poor old sods. It was only recently that they took the strips of sticky paper off the kitchen windows.

I tap the barometer and the glass and both hands fall off.

'Oh, bleeding marvellous,' hollers dad. 'You haven't been in the house two minutes and you've smashed a priceless work of art.'

'Come off it, dad. I only tapped it!'

'Well, don't tap it! It's not there to be tapped.'

'Everybody taps barometers, dad. It's like touching things when they've got a "wet paint" sign on them.'

'That's not the point. That had been there for two weeks without anything happening to it.'

'I can believe that. The needle was jammed at set-fair. That's why I tapped it.'

'You leave things alone that don't belong to you. You just leave things –'

Where this typically turgid argument would have led us I will never know because mum suddenly pops out of the front room all of a twitter.

'He's on,' she says. 'Come on! He's on.' She sees me and waves her hand. 'Oh, hello Timmy dear. You're just in time. Come on.' And she doubles back into the room. I am a spot choked because I always reckon on mum coming across with some of the human warmth that dad so obviously lacks. His milk of human kindness has to be reconstituted with draught bitter.

9

'What's up, dad?' I ask. 'Has mum got a crush on the bloke introducing Blue Peter.'

'No, it's Jason. I thought you knew.'

'Jason? Jason who?'

'Jason Noggett! Didn't you know that your nephew was appearing with Miss Mealie?'

'I didn't even know Miss Mealie was appearing. What's it all about, dad?'

Dad waves his hands in exasperation. 'Come and watch. Your mother will tell you.'

But mother is clearly not going to tell anybody anything, except to belt up. She is perched on the edge of her seat and bombarding her cakehole with Maltesers.

'Mum –'

'Sssh!'

'What –?'

'Sssh! Do be quiet!!'

Cut to the quick by this lack of parental interest, I adjust my peepers to the television set and listen to the disgusting tinkle, tinkle of 'Baa Baa Blacksheep' being picked out on a xylophone. As the sound fades, so a pretty female face fills the screen and a set of perfect gnashers split into a welcoming smile.

'Hello boys and girls,' says a voice of such cloying sweetness that I expect to see syrup leaking out of the volume control, 'are you ready for the music?' she pauses and nods, and to my disgust I find myself nodding back. 'That's good, because when it stops I'll be back here to introduce my little friends on Kiddichat. The programme where our panel of mini-viewers answer questions from you children at home. So, from me, Miss Mealie, it's: enjoy the music and see you in a minute.' She gives a sickening wave and fades out to make way for a bird in a ballet costume who does a little dance to the Dambusters' March, or some such popular melody. I wait hopefully for her to catch her toe in a crack between the floorboards, but it is not one of my lucky afternoons.

'Jason is on this lot?' I ask.

'Sssh,' says mum.

'Have you got a pin mum, my leg just fell off.'

'Ssh! !'

When Miss Mealie reappears, mum nearly topples off her chair she is leaning forward so far. 'There he is,' she squeals. 'There he is!'

I look over Miss Mealie's shoulder and it is indeed possible to recognise Sidney's first-born with his fingers stuck up his bracket in characteristic fashion. He is sitting at a table with three other kids.

'Our little Jason, a tele star,' breathes mum as if something with a halo round its bonce has started tapping on the window.

'What is it, mum, a nose-picking contest?'

'That's enough from you,' snaps mum and I have not heard her voice so sharp since she caught dad snogging with Ada Figgins in the Gents at The Highwayman on New Year's Eve. There can't be many blokes who have seen the new year in with a lavatory brush shoved down the front of their trousers.

'Why do they make them wear those stupid shirts,' I say conversationally. I would have done better to keep my trap shut.

'I sat up till three o'clock in the morning crocheting that,' sniffs mum. 'Rosie said that the producer thought it was "absolutely super".'

'I'm sorry mum, I –

'How many times have you been on tele, then, clever-shanks?' says mum accusingly.

'He nearly made Police Five a couple of times, though,' sneers dad.

It is disgusting isn't it? Rounding on their own flesh and blood because my mug has never had six hundred and twenty-five lines running through it. The way some people go on about the tele you would think it was some kind of new religion. Certainly not the old one because the only time you see dad move fast is to turn off the Epilogue. It is as if being exposed to a back to front collar for longer than five seconds was going to kill him.

I should tell them both to get stuffed but I am too

fascinated by the prospect of seeing what the infant Jason gets up to.

'Did you like the dance, Benedict?' says Miss Mealie engagingly.

Benedict must have been doing something else at the time because he gazes vacantly into the camera as if concentrating on a spot in the middle of it.

'How about you, Imogen? Imogen!' The name has to be repeated because Imogen seems totally engrossed in twisting the arm of the small boy next to her. He bursts into tears.

'Chinese burn,' says Imogen proudly.

'Come on, Eric,' pipes Miss Mealie. 'You wouldn't want the fairy to see you cry would you? Fairies only like brave boys.'

'They're keeping the camera off him,' hisses ma, incensed. 'I don't know what they've got against the child. It's always the same.'

'Probably waiting 'til he gets his finger out of his conk,' I say. Mum is so worked up she does not pay any attention to me.

'He's the life and soul of the whole programme,' she chokes. 'Everybody only watches to see him. There! Look at that.''

Jason has now succeeded in getting both his fingers stuck up his snoz and the camera quickly whips back to Miss Mealie.

'Is that all he does?' I say innocently.

'Don't be ridiculous,' snarls mum. 'It's not surprising, is it? Nobody talking to the child. Ooh! I wish I could get my hands on that woman. She's not as innocent as she looks, you know. Rosie's heard a few things about her. Oh, yes. I don't know why she has the little chap on the programme if she's only going to humiliate him.'

I tune out mum's drone and stare at Miss Mealie with fresh interest. She looks the kind of bird who is so simperingly awful that you want to shout 'knickers!' into her lug hole, but maybe I am doing her an injustice. Perhaps she is a bit of a raver on the quiet.

Eric stops crying when Miss M. quickly shoves a sweet in his miserable little cakehole and at last the camera settles on Noggett junior. The child star has now got his digits out of his hooter and mum coos with ecstasy.

'Oh, isn't he lovely?'

I turn away and look at dad who winces and shakes his head. I have a feeling that he finds the whole spectacle as nauseating as I do.

'So, now I can see that Jason is ready to answer our first question. You liked the dancing didn't you, Jason?'

Jason nods enthusiastically, and you can tell that he is a real chip off the old block. Another crawler.

'Yeth, Mith Mealie,' he lisps.

'Very well, Jason. Here is a question from Sandra Page, aged eight, of Mellow Meads, Wessex Way, South Dene. That does sound a nice place, doesn't it, Jason? Would you like to live there?'

Jason casts his eyes down and speaks in a thin, reedy treble. 'I want to stay at home with my mummy.'

What a pro! I bet that has them crying into their crackers down at the day nursery. Mum nearly bursts a gusset.

'What a nice thought,' says Miss Mealie, switching on full beam. 'Now, let's have that question. Sandra wants to know what time all the boys and girls on the panel go to bed. When do you go to bed, Jason?'

'When The Sand Man comes.'

'And when does he come?'

'When Dadda goes away. Then mummy says "You go to bed now, Jason, because mummy and The Sand Man want –" '

'Yes, well that does sound nice, doesn't it?' says Miss Mealie hurriedly.

' "– to be alone together," ' says Jason doggedly. 'And then sometimes uncle –'

'Imogen!' shrieks Miss Mealie, 'what time do you go to bed?'

'Depends what's on the tele,' says the pretty little mite, starting to chew a pencil she has been jabbing Eric with.

'If there is a film, I stay up until "bye, bye, light" time.'
' "Bye, bye light" time?'
'When the light runs away through the little hole in the middle of the tele, we say: "by, bye, light".'
'How sweet,' beams Miss M. 'You are grown up, aren't you? "Sand Men" and "bye, bye, lights" –'
'And uncles,' pipes up little Jason.
'He's a caution, isn't he,' says mum. 'I don't know where he gets these things from, I really don't.'

I was thinking the same about Rosie but I don't let on. Ever since she went to the Isla de Amori and started reading those women's lib. articles, she has been a different woman. The time was when she thought the sun shone through the slit in Sidney's Y-fronts. Now he is lucky if she can find the strength to chuck his smalls into the washing machine. I had not realised that her living in the Cromby Motel could create many of the problems that have been afflicting Sidney and myself. I must have a discreet word with her about it. Sidney does have a position to keep up and it is not only the one you find on page fifty-two of 'Everything you ever wanted to know about sex, but felt such a fool for asking.'

I get my chance to speak to Rosie sooner than I had expected, because she rolls up with the infant Noggett an hour later. By taxi, no less, and accompanied by a thin, long-haired git wearing a beard and a shiny leather jacket with coloured panels. He looks a right berk.

'Oh, mother,' trills Rosie, all posh-like. 'This is Dominic Ralph – he produces the show.'

'Charmed, I'm sure,' says mum, and she actually curtseys to the creep. Either that or her knicks have worked up.

'Sooper,' says Dominic, taking one of mum's hands with both of his – he probably needs two to lift it – 'absolutely soopah. You've got a very talented little grandson here. Is this the proud father?'

He beams at me and I am quick to look disgusted. Likewise mum and Rosie.

'Oh, no,' says Rosie with a light laugh. 'This is my brother.'

'Timmy,' I say. 'Pleased to meet you.'

'How do you do.' Dominic nods and his hair flops over his forehead.

'Dominic's going to take me out for a bite to discuss the new series,' says Rosie, avoiding my eyes. 'I wonder if you'd mind putting Jason to bed, mum. I won't be back late.'

'There's some football on tele tonight, Jason,' I say eagerly. 'Would you like to watch it with Uncle Timmy?' I mean, if you can't lick them, join them. That's my motto.

'No,' says the ungrateful little bleeder, without looking at me. 'Have you got any thweeties, grandma?'

'Yes, dear. When you've had your supper.'

'Don't want any supper! I want thweeties!' Jason's fat little lip – it would be a darn sight fatter if I had my way – starts quivering and he turns on his mother. 'You promised!'

'Yes, all right dear.' Rosie looks at mum. 'He is a bit over-tired tonight, mum. Maybe if you did give him a few sweets and put him to bed.'

'Remember to clean those little toothie-pegs first,' I beam. 'We don't want nasty old Giant Decay rotting them away and causing little Jason excruciating agony, do we?'

'Are you trying to terrify the child,' says Rosie angrily. 'A few sweets aren't going to hurt him.'

'Uncle Timmy was only thinking of little Jason's welfare,' I say.

Dominic looks at me thoughtfully. 'Uncle Timmy,' he says.

'What?' Rosie's expression is like that of a cat seeing another moggy approaching its food bowl.

'He's got a kind face. It might be rather nice. Round off the show.'

'What do you mean?' Mum looks from face to face inquiringly.

15

'Have you ever had any acting experience?' asks Dominic.

'No. Well, I mean, I've done a lot of work like acting. I've been a Holiday Host in a holiday camp and a salesman.'

'Soopah, soopah.' Dominic extends a hand and pats me on the wrist. It occurs to me that Sidney may have nothing to worry about tonight. I reckon the last bird Dominic fancied was probably his mum.

'You've never done any acting in your life!' quibbles Rosie.

'I've done as much as Conk Digits here,' I say. 'Just because I haven't been to Rada doesn't mean I haven't got talent.'

'Pop along and see me,' says Dominic transferring the pressure to my upper arms. 'No promises, but it might be interesting.'

'Are you going to put him on the tele?' says mum, catching up with the action at last. 'Oh Timmy, I always knew you had it in you.'

A couple of days later I am sitting at the back of the Studio Five Control Room, waiting for Miss Mealie and the rest of them to come out of Make-up.

'You'll get the feel of the show up here, ducky,' breezes Dominic Ralph. 'Just let it flow all over you and I'll introduce you to a few people afterwards. That chair comfy enough for you? Goodo! Ah, Melly my darling. How is our lovely girlikin today?'

'Pissed off!' snarls Miss Mealie, grinding out a lipstick covered snout in the centre of a half eaten sandwich. 'If you think I'm going to hang about while those vicious little vermin have their tacky curls lacquered, you've got another think coming. Who's the star of this show?'

'You are of course, darling. There's never one shadow of doubt about it.'

'And while we're about it, we could do with some new kids. I don't anticipate that we'd get anything better but at least we'd have a change of mother. Those greedy, grasping, status-seeking harridans are beginning to drive

16

me insane.' Miss M. produces a small container and swallows a couple of pills. She shudders. 'Christ! But these things taste disgusting. Just getting them past my gums makes me want to throw up.'

'Melly,' says Dominic hurriedly. 'I'd like you to meet Timothy Lea. His nephew is on the programme.'

'Oh dear,' says Miss M., gushingly, 'me and my big mouth. Please don't take offence. I don't mean a word I say. I'm just a bit overwrought at the moment. Let me guess which one is yours. Imogen perhaps? No! Of course not, not with that colouring. Jason? Yes, it must be Jason. He's so good-looking.'

I know she is bull-shitting but I cannot help blushing. That upper-class voice does not help either. I am a push-over for a posh bint.

'Yes, it's Jason,' I say. 'Rosie Noggett is my sister.'

'Yes. Very pretty blonde girl. She wasn't one of the ones I was referring to, of course.'

'Funny. It sounded just like her,' I say.

'Oh, you naughty boy,' Miss M. waggles a finger at me. 'You mustn't try to make me feel any worse than I do. Ah, here they come."

Rosie and the rest of the mums and brats crowd into the control room and Miss M. starts behaving like Miss Mealie. She is a very good-looking brunette with a few more lines than you see on the tele. I read her as being about twenty-eight, five foot six and a half and 36c cup.

'Miss Mealie and panel into the studio please,' says Dominic. '*Please* don't play with those switches, boys. And, Imogen dear, that's not a very good place to put your chewing gum, is it? Give it to mummy, there's a good girl. And mummies, could we have absolute quiet during this show please? We're always interested in your comments but we'd like them when we're off the air.'

'Look into the camera and don't stutter, Benedict,' hisses one mother. 'Remember there's that series coming up.'

'Don't kiss me, Rupert,' says another, 'you'll smudge your make-up.'

When you see the expression of grim determination on these women's mugs you can understand what Miss Mealie is getting at. They look like Olympic swimming coaches.

'Good luck, Jason,' I say. 'Don't forget your sweets.'

'Shut up, you!' snaps the little monster, snatching them from my hand. 'You shouldn't be here.'

Little do you know, I think. A couple of weeks and you could be one of the youngest has-beens in the business. I can see myself telling him the bad news: 'Sorry about this, Jason, but you'll have to make way for a younger child. The public wants youth, you know.'

'But Uncle Timmy!'

'No buts, Jason. You're finished. Pack your dolly mixtures and get out!'

I watch the little basket gobble down another handful of sweets as he takes his place on the set, and try to shut out the canvas chair with his name on the back of it. A couple of hours in this place and you can feel all washed up at the age of twenty-two.

'On set everybody, please,' repeats Dominic. 'We're on the air in two minutes.'

'Can I have his autograph when he learns to write?' I say as I sit down next to Rosie.

'Shut up, jealous!' she barks.

Dominic starts speaking soothing words into a microphone that connects with the set and a shapely bint by his side starts giving a countdown. In front of us are a row of television screens and a bloke on Dominic's right commands a bank of switches which control the pictures on each screen. I can see Jason's self-satisfied little mug staring at me in horrible close-up. At least he seems to be able to leave his hooter alone this week.

'You blocked up his nostrils, did you?' I say to Rosie.

'Shut up!!'

'Have you got my pills, darling?' Miss Mealie's voice comes through to the control box. 'I left them on the desk.'

'Don't seem to be here, darling.' A slight edge creeps into Dominic's voice. 'Twenty-five seconds to go. Let's

18

have a good show now everybody. Good luck.'

'Fifteen, fourteen, thirteen –' The Production Assistant's voice drones on sounding professionally bored.

I look back to the monitor with Jason's mug on it and watch the little swine slotting another peppermint into his cakehole. Hey, wait a minute! Those are not sweets! With a sense of impending horror I recognise Miss Mealie's pills. The ones she said tasted so horrible. They could probably kill Jason. And in front of millions of viewers too!

'Those pills!' I shout.

'Ssh!!!'

'Jason is eating Miss Mealie's pills!'

'Good afternoon boys and girls. And mummies and daddies too –' Miss Mealie's honeyed tones fill the silent control room.

'Are they dangerous?'

We all peer at the monitor screen with Jason in it.

'He's looking a bit green.'

'– sick.'

'– blinking.'

'– awful.'

'– stomach pump.'

'We'll have to take him off when the song comes up.'

'But every moment is precious. You can't leave him there!'

'It's a matter of seconds –'

'No!!'

'There's the other kiddies to be considered too. If you take him off, just like that, it's going to disturb them,' sniffs one of the other mums.

'You'd rather he dropped dead, I suppose!' Rosie is moving towards the door.

'Ladies, please!'

'You leave that door alone!'

'He doesn't look so bad now.'

'Get out of my way, you slagheap!!'

'Ooh, that's nice, isn't it? I can see where your little boy gets his manners from.'

19

'– and now children, here's a lovely song that you all know very well.'

'– fingers up his nose.'

'Ladies please ! !'

'– perming a little kiddy's hair.'

'– looks more natural than yours ! '

'Baggage ! '

'Slut ! ! '

And, so help me, all the mums start bashing the living daylights out of each other. Dominic and his assistants are spreadeagled protectively over their switches while Rose is trying to get into the studio with the rest of the mothers holding her back. Rising above this unseemly din can be heard the strains of 'Dance to your Daddy, My Little Laddie' sung by a very fat gentleman with a paunch so large that it looks as if he would have great difficulty getting into a position from which to achieve parenthood.

As always in situations like this I do not know what to do. To break into the studio seems like running stark naked into the audience chamber of The Vatican shouting 'The Pope's a Jew ! ' and the sight of birds indulging in a punch-up freezes me to the marrow. The shenanigans in the control room are not going unnoticed by our studio panel and I am reassured about the state of Jason's health when I see his face split into a wide grin at the sight of Rosie swiping another mum around the kisser with her handbag. Only Miss Mealie is looking disturbed and I can see that Ralph must be able to contact her because she suddenly leaps up and tries to snatch the pills from Jason's hands. Jason is not the kind of lad to take this treatment lying down and from what I can see on the central monitor screen, part two of the programme opens with the interesting sight of Miss Mealie and one of her little charges wrestling across the desk.

'Dey my sweeties ! My sweeties ! ' screeches the treacherous little Jason. 'My Uncle Timmy gave them to me.'

'You swine ! ' Rosie rounds on me immediately. 'You'd stop at nothing to get on that programme, wouldn't you?'

'Now, Rosie, don't be ridiculous —'

'Poison your own nephew!'

'Rosie. It was an accident. I thought they were the kid's sweets. They haven't done him any harm. Look!'

Miss Mealie has succeeded in wresting the pills from Jason and is quick to shove a couple past her own sensuous lips. No doubt she needs them. 'Um, delicious!' she pipes. 'Would you like one of mine?'

Before Jason can think about it she pushes a packet of gob-stoppers along the desk and little Greedy Guts is on them like a flash. He is obviously the same stickler for principle as his dad.

'There, that's all right then, isn't it?' I say, relieved. Miss Mealie clearly thinks so too.

'Right, now here's a question from Pauline Rogers of Twenty-four Crowmart Lane, Dagenham. She wants to know what the panel's daddies do when they come home in the evening. Who would like to answer that one? Jason?'

But Jason is not expressing a willingness to answer any questions. He now is looking very thoughtful and Miss Mealie has to probe. 'I expect you're glad to see Daddy when he comes home in the evenings. What do you do?' She leans forward expectantly and Jason clears his throat and vomits all over the desk.

CHAPTER TWO

'You mustn't blame yourself,' says Miss Mealie.

'I think it made the whole programme very relevant,' says Dominic soothingly. 'It was terribly "now". That's what television is all about.'

We are in the saloon bar of the pub opposite the studio having what Dominic calls an 'unwinding drinkypoo' and I am wondering if one is going to be enough to get out all the twists.

'Does your sister often behave like that?' asks Miss Mealie.

'You mean like when she threw me through the glass window?'

'I was thinking of when she tried to strangle you with the microphone lead.'

'She took evening classes in Karate. That's where she got the technique, she always had the temper.'

'Remarkable. I sometimes think these programmes bring out the worst in the mothers.'

'They don't do a lot for the kiddies either,' I say, gingerly rubbing the ankle that Jason tried to separate from the rest of my leg.

'I won't miss him,' says Miss Mealie with feeling. 'I don't think I offend you too much when I say that?'

'Oh no,' I agree, 'I wouldn't miss him if I was looking down the sights of a rifle.'

Miss M. takes another hefty swig at her brandy and I signal for the barman to repair it.

'He has some very nasty habits. He never went to the toilet, you know. When we came to check his locker we found out why.'

'We had the same trouble with the broom cupboard at home,' I say. 'Mum used to think it was the cat. She belted the living daylights out of the poor bleeder.'

'What have you got on tonight, Timmy?' says Dominic

suddenly, giving me one of those funny looks, as if he means in the underwear line.

'Well, I – er,' Miss Mealie is screwing up her eyes in a 'don't do it, buster' grimace, 'I'm going out with one of my mates,' I lie. Miss Mealie nods approvingly.

'I thought of having a few people round for drinks,' says Dominic expansively. 'Why don't you and your friend drop in?'

'I think he's got tickets for something,' I gulp.

'Well, afterwards then.'

'If we don't get out too late. Ta very much.'

Dominic's eyes narrow. 'I hope you'll be able to make it,' he says firmly. 'I want to get this situation regarding the new format straightened out as soon as possible. With us having to replace young Noggett it's a good moment to introduce a new face at the head of the table.' He looks at Miss Mealie whose smile is about as natural as a set of orange peel gnashers.

'Jason is definitely out, is he?' I ask trying to conceal my satisfaction.

'Definitely. He's lost the public's confidence. They can accept what happened but they won't want to bite their nails down to the quick waiting for a repetition. It's not fair on the child, either.'

'Indeed, no,' I say, shaking my head gravely.

'I must be off,' says Dominic giving my arm a squeeze. 'I've got to chill the crème de menthe. Do hope you will be able to look in later. It will definitely be worth your while. And – er, do bring your friend, there'll be lots of people. Forty-seven Carmarthen Mews. You won't forget it, will you?' He gives a little wink and practically dances out of the pub.

'The place is riddled with them,' says Miss Mealie disapprovingly, before he is out of earshot.

'U-mm,' I say. It is occurring to me that I might be on the outskirts of a dicey situation. Dominic Ralph may well have a scrambled hormone balance but he is in a position to turn me into a tele star. As the solution to any sexual hang-ups that I feel in the next few minutes, Miss Mealie has a much bigger future, but she is obviously not sobbing with gratitude about the prospect of sharing the billing with Uncle Timmy. Maybe I had better keep the demon lust under control tonight and slip round for an arm distance chat with Dominic later.

'I never meet a real man these days,' says Miss Mealie, running her finger round the rim of her glass. 'Only poufs and snotty little kids.'

'Don't you like children?' I say innocently, sliding her glass towards her.

'Are you kidding. Hey – did you hear that? Joke.'

'Fantastic,' I say.

'The only thing I hate more than kids is mothers. But then you know that. Do you know what I like?'

'No,' I lie to her.

She leans forward and whispers in my ear. 'Does that shock you?'

'These days, nothing shocks me. It's funny though, isn't it? You liking that though you don't like kids.'

'It never occurred to me to consider that there might be a connection until you mentioned it. It's like being told that filling a fountain pen makes babies.'

'Yes,' I say. I am coming to the conclusion that Miss Mealie is well on the way to becoming very successfully pissed. This, of course, is sad but not so sad that I am going to lose any sleep about it. In fact I may well be able to use it as the framework of a very pleasant evening. If I take Miss Mealie home and put her to bed – and at a pinch myself – I can then go on to Dominic's and seal my star status over a pitcher of crème de menthe.

'You were lucky you managed to talk your way out of going to Dominic's place,' says Miss Mealie, colliding with my thoughts. 'It's a very kinky set-up. I don't know who he's living with at the moment but it's quite awful, the things that go on there. I know that what people do in the privacy of their own homes is their own affair – or affairs – hey, did you hear that? I made another joke.'

'Great.'

'Well, laugh when I make a joke. Haven't you got a sense of humour?'

'I laugh a lot inside.'

'You should let it bubble to the surface a little more often. Anyway, where was I?'

'You were saying I should laugh more.'

'No! Stupid. I was telling you about Dominic's flat. I was saying how awful it is. You're – er, not like that, are you?'

'As a clockwork orange. Why do you think I've got this far with Dominic? There's a kind of chemistry between us.'

'Don't be stupid! I can tell them a mile off. There's nothing queer about you.'

'I don't think you should say that without proof.'

'Are you serious? You're having me on, aren't you? You think you can talk me into taking you into my bed so that I can prove that you're not queer.'

'I'm confused already. Let's just go to bed.'

'You're cool, aren't you?'

'You told me what you liked.'

'I didn't say anything about you.'

'That would have been forward.'

Miss Mealie is now walking up the buttons of my shirt with her fingers. She gets to the collar, clambers over my chin, tramples on my lips and ends up on my nose. 'Bite off your nose!' she says gaily.

'Let me take you home,' I husk.

Five minutes later she has made a telephone call and I have poured – and pawed – her into a taxi. This evening had better come to something because it is costing me a fortune. There was a time when a bird could reckon she was in for a good time if I ordered a Babycham and two straws.

'Oh, I'm feeling a sleepy girl,' murmurs Miss M. snuggling up to me in the back of the taxi. Not long before I can say the same, I think to myself and try not to watch the meter ticking up. By the cringe, but it seems to move faster than the last column on a posh mileometer. At this rate I am going to have to thumb a lift home.

Home. The word makes me feel nervous. Even as I sit here mum and Rosie are probably propping a vat of boiling oil above the front door. Jason's golden future in ruins and all because Uncle Timmy slipped him a phial of Micky Phinns. That is what they are going to believe anyway, and little rat fink Jason is not going to come to nunky's aid. Maybe it would be a good idea to steer clear of the ancestral pile for a few days. Until I am an established star in my own right. Once my mug appears on the screen, mum at least will forgive all.

'Here we are, mate,' says the taxi driver.

'It's right next to the tube!' I say aggrieved.

'Yeah. You want me to move it into the middle of Hyde Park for you?'

'It would have been just as quick by tube.'

'Yeah, well you're here now, Rockerfeller. There's a pie stall round the corner if you want to take the lady out to dinner.'

'Are we there?' says Miss Mealie, waking up.

''Ere! I know you don't I?' says the cabby, registering Miss Mealie's face. 'You're on the tele, aren't you? My kiddies all watch your programme.'

'How nice,' says Miss M.

'Yeah. And my little Trampas has got a birthday next week. Do you reckon you could read out his name?'

'Drop me a postcard at the studio and I'll see what I can do.' Miss Mealie delivers a royal smile and sweeps into the block of flats. The taxi driver is so bowled over that he does not even examine the miserably small tip I have given him.

'She's a lady, that one,' he says, looking me up and down as if I am not fit to dust her microphone lead.

'A real pro.' I agree with him and follow Miss M. into the flat. This kind of reverence could become habit-forming. I cannot think why I have never considered show-biz before.

'"Trampas"! Did you hear that?' sniffs Miss M. when

I join her in the lift. 'We had one mother write in whose brat was called Ajax.'

'He might have been named after the football team.'

'I don't think so. We got a letter about his sister next week. She was called Vimia.' Miss Mealie shudders. 'God, but I need a drink. You're coming in, are you?'

Try and stop me, I think. The investment I have made this evening should entitle me to a season ticket.

We leave the lift and walk down a corridor long enough to house a rifle range before stopping outside a door with two hundred and forty-seven on it. I am feeling the excitement I feel before the start of a football match. I know what to do, it is just a question of manoeuvring myself into a position to do it. Miss Mealie inserts her key and pushes open the door. Very nice too. Lots of polished wood furniture and spotlights, and a thick white carpet.

'Nice place you've got here,' I say, 'and here – and here.'

'Down, tiger.' Miss M. disentangles herself from my probing fingers. 'Let's have a drink first.'

'I like the 'first'. That must be a good sign.

'What would you like?' she says.

'Scotch would be fine.'

'Ice, water?'

'Just water, thanks.'

She wanders into the kitchen and I take a look round the flat. The bedroom particularly catches my eye. A low double bed in the centre of the room with a multicoloured patchwork counterpane. In the ceiling above is a circular mirror.

'Do you like my bedroom?' says Miss M., appearing beside me with my drink.

'Fantastic. I didn't imagine you in a place like this.'

'I suppose you thought I lived in a bed-sit with a tabby cat and a pile of Beatrix Potters.'

'Uum,' I say, not quite certain what a Beatrix Potter is.

'Tell me about yourself,' says Miss M. lounging gracefully across a low divan. 'What do you do for a living?'

'Nothing at the moment.'

'Resting? How very theatrical.'

'I was working with my brother-in-law flogging cleaners, but we've packed that in now. I've done a number of things on and off. I worked in a hotel and at a holiday camp. And I was a driving instructor at one time. The first real job I ever had was cleaning windows.'

'Cleaning windows! That must have been interesting.' Miss Mealie's eyes contain more promises than a Turkish Delight commercial.

'Yes. It did have its moments.'

'It's funny you should have been a window cleaner because I have a friend who is looking for one at the moment. Justin Tymely. Maybe you've heard of him?' I shake my head. 'No? Well there's no reason why you should have, I suppose. He's a bit of a wheeler-dealer in the art-film world and he's making a little epic which has some window-cleaning episodes in it. Maybe I can put you in touch?'

'Yes please.'

Miss Mealie delves in her bag and draws out a crumpled card. 'Yes, here we are. Tell him I suggested you got in touch.'

I look at the card which says 'Justin Tymely—Managing Director, Trion Productions', with an address and two telephone numbers. Very impressive. At last my luck is changing. Not only a famous tele personality but a star of the silver screen as well. I wonder if she knows anyone in radio? I just hope that success does not spoil me. Anyhow I must not think of myself all the time. This Leacrazy bird is obviously waiting for me to make love to her so she can boast about it to all her friends.

'You're very beautiful,' I say, leaning forward and gently removing the glass from her unresisting fingers. I spill a bit on the carpet, but I don't think she notices.

'Thank you,' she says. 'So are you.'

'You don't have to say that,' I murmur.

'You knew already, didn't you?'

'Kiss me,' I say hurriedly and dive onto her lips, carefully tucking the glass away under the divan. Her lips are soft as rose petals and she kisses in a continuous nibbling motion, like half a dozen minnows attacking a piece of bread paste.

'You smell nice,' she says, when we come up for air. 'Let's go into the bedroom.'

'I smell even nicer in bedrooms,' I murmur, kissing her on the ear and thinking that it is no wonder that Cary Grant has given up making pictures. Poor old sod, what chance does he have with blokes like me around?

Miss Mealie takes me by the hand like I am one of her tiny charges and leads me to the bedroom. We stop by the patchwork counterpane and her fingers slide round to the small of my back. She eases out my black, Captain Whiplash, tapered, slim-fit, see-through, pure silk shirt and purrs contentedly as her fingers make contact with my bare flesh. I cannot blame her. I would probably react in the same way if I was touching myself for the first time.

There are thirty-eight buttons on the front of her long gingham dress. I know because I count them one by one as I unpop down from neck to navel while we trade kisses like they pay five pounds a hundred. She is wearing one of those half-cup bras which is so shallow it looks more like a saucer and her breasts swell over the top like the heads of a couple of glasses of stout.

'Hello, Uncle Timmy,' she breathes, ruffling the hair at the back of my neck and driving against my lips like she is trying to find a permanent anchorage. 'Here's to a mutually stimulating relationship.'

'I'll drink to that,' I murmur, 'and what better vessel than your own beautiful mouth?' I kiss her tenderly and gently tug the dress off her shoulders so that it starts its long descent towards floor level. My God, but it is beautiful! If they gave Oscars for this kind of thing, I would need a fork-lift truck to carry mine away. Miss Mealie obviously thinks so too because she is quick to brush away the hands that fumble for my own shirt buttons.

'Cool it, stud,' she breathes. 'I hate to see a man doing a woman's job. Just relax and let Auntie Mealie take the strain.'

One of the old school, obviously, I think as I allow myself to be pushed back onto the bed. I gaze up at the circular mirror and enjoy the sight of my new friend spilling kisses down my chest as she swiftly unbuttons my nifty dicky dirt.

'You have a magnificent body,' she breathes.

'U-um,' I murmur. Well! It sounds conceited to agree with her, doesn't it? Yet on the other hand there is no reason why I should perjure myself for the sake of modesty. 'You're not bad yourself,' I say, trying to be kind, but she is too busy dismantling the front of my trousers to pay much attention. The way she grabs hold of the zip on my flies, you would think she was going to wrench it straight down to the turn-ups. I try to grab a handful of knockers that happen to be swinging in my direction but again she brushes me aside. 'Relax baby,' she coos, 'this is my party.'

'Tell me when there's a game we can both play.'

'I'll call you when it's time to blow out the candles.'

I lie back to think about that one and feel relieved that I have put on a clean pair of socks as they join my shoes on the floor by the bed.

Gazing up into the mirror I can see what Miss Mealie was on about. It is amazing that I can walk down the street without being savaged by Lea-hungry bints. The frustration some of those poor birds must have to endure when they turn their mince pies loose on my six foot one and a half inches of man-mountain grandeur, does not bear thinking about.

'And now –' Biting her lip in honest ecstasy, Miss Mealie seizes the top of my jockey briefs and proceeds to steer them over the not inconsiderable obstacle that my own passionate nature has placed in her way. I can excuse her clumsiness because I realise that this is probably the most exciting thing that has ever happened to her.

Seconds later I am spread out upon the bed like a patient anaesthetised upon a table, naked and waiting for the action.

'Oh baby, start operating,' I grunt.

But, to my amazement, Miss Mealie starts doing up

the buttons on her dress. 'What's the matter?' I say, raising myself onto an elbow. 'Are you cold, or something?'

Miss Mealie shakes her head mockingly. ' "Or something",' she says. 'Don't move, I always want to remember you like that.' And then, she tears her dress open so that buttons explode all over the floor, slaps her face a couple of times and starts screaming.

'Rape! Help! Murder! Rape! Rape! Rape!'

I find this very interesting. I mean, it is a bit strange, isn't it? One minute she is all over me and the next it is me all over. Maybe it turns her on to feel that she is being raped. Yes, that must be it. She seems a very passionate girl. I do not mind playing along with her little fantasy if it makes her – and me – happy.

'Help! Help! Rape!'

If she is going to be like this before I have even touched her, God knows what she will be like in the sack. The prospect launches me from the bed and I close with her fast.

'Don't touch me!'

She starts running through the living room and I follow. I hope the walls are thick because her language would make a Billingsgate porter switch off his deaf aid. I catch up with her by the door but before I can deter her she has flung it open.

'Rape! Help!' she screams and runs out into the corridor. I get as far as the doorway and then stop. I mean! There is a limit. I don't mind a quick frisk round the apartment but chasing her round the block in the altogether could lead to trouble. People are not as liberated as you read in the papers.

Just as I am making up my mind what to do next, Miss Mealie returns. But she is not alone. She is sobbing hysterically on the arm of a tall fellow with a flashlight camera in his hand. Another guy follows on behind with a notepad in his mitt.

'Thank God you came!' sobs Miss M. hysterically. 'It was horrible. Horrible!'

'What are you rabbiting on about?' I say angrily.

'How did he get in?' says the fellow with the notepad, pencil poised.

'I invited him up to discuss the show and then – and then –' Miss M. starts sobbing convulsively.

'He is in the show, is he?'

Miss M.'s sobs stop immediately. 'He was going to be. That's what I wanted to discuss.'

'I've never heard such a load of cobblers in my life!' I say indignantly. 'She invited me up to her flat and into her bedroom, and then she took all my clothes off.'

'I can see you put up a fight,' says the bloke with the camera, taking a shot of me.

'Was he naked like that when he came into the flat?' says the one with the note pad.

'No. He said he wanted to use the toilet and then – and then –' More sobs soak the carpet.

'Tore your dress, did he?'

'She tore her dress!' I yelp.

All the time the fellow with the camera is snapping away like it was some kind of still-life class he has blundered across.

'What are you two guys doing up here, anyway?' I say, beginning to smell a rat – or more likely, three of the little furry chaps.

'We're freelance reporters. We were coming to do an article on Miss Mealie.'

'You've got quite a scoop then,' I say sarcastically. 'Too bad Miss Mealie won't let you use it.'

'What do you mean?' says the lady in question.

'It must be obvious. If a kid can get thrown off the programme for puking his ring, then they're going to crucify you for having a nasty naked man in your room. Even if your lousy story was true, some mud would stick. Now, why don't you wise up and send these two goons back to wherever it is they come from?' It would sound better if I borrowed Humphrey Bogart's mac for the delivery, but even then it might not cut much ice with Miss Mealie.

'Good thinking, rapist,' she hisses, 'but what makes you believe I want to stay on Kiddichat for the rest of my life?

There are other forms of entertainment, you know.'

And then I see it all. In a blinding flash it comes to me like a clip from an old detergent commercial. I have been framed. Miss Mealie is after publicity at any price and my career has been sacrificed to get it. I snatch at the camera but the geezer is too quick for me.

'Uh, uh. Naughty!' He wags a finger at me. 'If you want to see the pictures, buy the morning papers tomorrow.'

CHAPTER THREE

'This is a nice one of Timmy,' says mum. 'You can't see a lot of his face though.'

'You can't have everything,' says Dad, all sarcastic like.

They are studying the daily newspapers and I have made the front page of every one of them except *The Times* and the *Guardian*. I know that because mum has rushed out to buy everything except the *Jewish Chronicle* and *Chicks Own*. She is dead narky about my non-appearance in the quality press because she had to go up to Clapham South tube station before she found a copy.

Her reaction to my little spot of bother is interesting. Distress, accompanied by pride in the number of column inches I have achieved – I hasten to add that I am referring to space in the newspapers. Already she has the scissors out and I can see that I am taking over from Jason as the family star. Unfortunately my career now seems likely to be considerably shorter than that of the squint-eyed little monster glaring at me over his bowl of Tasty Frosties.

'You see where tangling with that harpy got you,' sniffs Rosie, who does not hate me quite so much now that she knows I am not destined for the Uncle Timmy spot.

'It was strictly a no-tangle action, I'm afraid, Rosie. You don't want to believe everything you read in the papers . . .'

'Oh yeah. Sounds very likely doesn't it,' says dad. 'Stark bollock naked and her with her dress half torn off. Nothing remarkable about that, is there? Oh dear me no.'

'She led me on, dad. I've never had to resort to force yet. It's not my nature.'

'She was a hussy, that one,' says Rosie helpfully. 'There was always a lot of talk about her.'

'I think she left those pills there on purpose,' I say,

seeing a chance to patch things up with Rosie. 'She never liked little Jason, did she?'

'She never liked anyone except herself.'

'It says here she's considering a number of film roles,' says mum, who is still studying the papers. 'She wants to be an all-round entertainer. There's talk of her going to Hollywood.'

'More like Neasden Rep.' snorts Rosie. 'She can't do anything.'

'Don't look at me, dad,' I say. 'I never found out.'

Most of the papers treat the affair as a put-up job and the police reaction has been less enthusiastic than that of firemen being called out to a false alarm at a water works. When I have read the dailies it occurs to me that I am being a bit premature in writing myself off for a job with Dominic Ralph. The worst headline is 'Was it Rape or a Lovers' Tiff?' Most of the others look on the funny side in a way that makes me wish I could have shared their merriment at the time. All in all it occurs to me that I might give Dominic a ring and see where I stand.

In fact I do not stand, I grovel. And even that does not do any good. I ring Dominic at the studio where no one can find him, and at his flat where the phone is answered in an accent that makes Kenneth Williams sound like Richard Roundtree.

'Who is that?' minces the voice. 'I'll just see if he's still in.' Pause. 'No, I'm most terribly sorry but he's just popped out. Can I take a message?'

'Yes,' I snarl. 'Tell him to turn off his bleeding electric razor. I can hardly hear what you're saying!' I jam down the receiver and compose myself to plan my next move.

I am not getting anywhere particularly fast when I light upon the card that the hated Miss Mealie gave me. This is probably another load of rubbish but anything is worth pursuing in my present situation. The first number on the card rings without reply, but the second is answered instantly.

'Dukley, Barchester and Rideabout,' says a very toffee-nosed voice, 'gee-ood morning.'

'I'm sorry, I've got the wrong number,' I say, 'I was after Trion Productions.'

'Justin Tymely?'

'That's right.'

'He's on the floor at the moment, shooting.' Blimey! I think, she's very cool about it. I wonder why I cannot hear any shots.

'I'll ring the police,' I say. The receiver is half an inch from the rest when I hear squawking coming from it.

'What are you talking about?' says the upper-crust voice tightly. 'He's shooting a film at the Sheppertree Studios!'

'Oh, silly me,' I say. 'I thought – oh well, it doesn't matter. I'll see him there. If you have any contact with him, tell him a window cleaner rang.'

'Don't go down to the studio,' says the bird exasperatedly, 'we need you here. The windows are filthy.'

'I'm not a real window cleaner,' I say. 'Well, I am, but not at the moment. I'm an actor window cleaner, Timothy Lea.'

'I'll tell him you're coming if he rings in, Mr. Lea,' says the voice icily and the line goes dead.

I am looking forward to visiting a real live film studio but by the time I get to what seems like the other end of the Home Counties, my enthusiasm is waning a bit. The buildings that greet my eye look like derelict hangars and I have not seen anything less impressive since I worked at Melody Bay Holiday Camp.

'Mr. Tymely,' I say to the peak-capped geezer on the gate. 'Mr. Justin Tymely. He's a film director.'

'What's he doing?'

'I don't know. Something with a window cleaner in it.'

The gatekeeper shakes his head and consults a list pinned beside his hatch. ' "Up the Ladder, Jack",' he says finally. 'Does that ring a bell?'

'Probably what I want. Where do I find him?'

'Straight down as far as you can go, then turn right, second left.'

Fifteen minutes later I find myself outside a metal sliding door with 'Stage 5' painted on it. There is also a red light and a sign which says 'Do not enter when light is flashing'. The light is flashing so I wait obediently. Five minutes pass and it has just started to rain when two youngish men come round the corner. They are dressed in painters' overalls and for a moment I make the stupid mistake of thinking that they are painters. Their conversation soon disabuses me.

'So I said to him I says, "If Crispin is going to have one then I'm going to have one". Well, I mean, it's ridiculous, isn't it?'

'And what did he say?'

'Stupid old faggot didn't know what I was talking about. Can you imagine? Ooh, I could have sunk my nails into him. Sink! Sink! Sink! I know you say I over-react to things –'

'I never said that! That I did never say. I said you were sensitive.'

'Well then!'

My contact with the conversation vanishes as the newcomers ignore the red light and disappear into the hangar. There is obviously no point in waiting about outside so I depress the lever and go in after them.

'Oiy! Can't you read?'

I am being addressed by a large red-faced man wearing a dirty plaid shirt and paint-spattered trousers.

'I'm sorry. I was following those two.'

'Sssh!!!' hiss the two gay blades who are now scowling at me as if I have started cracking walnuts under my arm during a palace reception.

'You use your eyes!' says the big man.

I nod vigorously and upon enquiring after Mr. Tymley's whereabouts, am directed round the back of what looks like a hastily erected pre-fabricated shed. This must be the set, I think to myself and peer through one of the windows with interest. A pretty, long-haired blonde girl wearing a mini skirt is being embraced by yet another man dressed in painter's overalls. As my pulse quickens he slides his hand inside the girl's blouse and begins massaging one of her breasts as if he is trying to smooth it into her chest. Saucy! I think to myself. Obviously Mr. Tymely makes a pretty explicit movie even by modern standards. The girl opens her eyes, sees me and gives a little yelp.

'Ooh, Ron!' she says.

Ron turns on me angrily. 'Bugger off!' he says. 'Go on, hop it before I give you a thick lip! Bleeding peeping toms!'

'I'm sorry,' I say urgently. 'I thought –' But there does not seem a lot of mileage in telling Ron what I thought, so I leave him and his lady friend to get better acquainted and push on to an intersection between piles of props ranging from choir stalls to bar fittings. This, at last, must be where the action is, because I can actually see a camera. Standing beside it is a greasy-haired individual with cheeks and chest like a retired pouter pigeon that has gone to bird seed. He is shaking his head at a tall, slim young man who has a mane of hair flowing from half way down the back of his head, the upper part of that article being bald as an egg. The tall geezer is wearing faded denim from head to toe and has an expensive-looking silk scarf bulging from his neck.

'All right, all right,' shouts Lofty,'Sellotape her nipples! Jesus Christ, isn't there a woman in the whole of London who can erect her nipples. When the hell are we going to get something in the can?'

'Jim,' says Greasebonce, 'do her nipples, will you?' Jim is playing cards with half a dozen painters and stagehands and seems irritated at being disturbed.

'Oh, bleeding heck,' he says, throwing down his cards. 'That's extra, you know, Sellotaping nipples. Extra.' He drags himself to his feet and advances onto the set.

'Bloody unions,' snarls Greasebonce under his breath in a gruff Scottish accent. 'Most of these bastards want danger money before they'll pull the bog chain.'

The set is obviously intended to represent the inside of a bedroom and the lady now complaining about Jim's cold hands is wearing a black lace negligee and one of the biggest sets of knockers I have ever seen. Cleaning his nails on the other side of the rumpled bed is a queer looking cove in the inevitable painters' overalls. He managed to make them look like the latest male fashion dreamed up by one of those kinky French designers.

'Right. Thank you, Jim,' says Lofty. 'Now, Mac, if you've got some film in the camera, let's do it again. And for God's sake, Crispin, put a bit of life into it! Try and imagine Sandra is a man or something.'

'Charming!' says Sandra.

'You're supposed to be a lusty housepainter about to enjoy the sexual experience of a lifetime,' continues Lofty. 'At the moment it sounds as if you've popped in to ask for a glass of water because you've come over a little queer.'

'He should be so lucky,' mutters Mac.

'If you don't like my reading, Justin, I don't know why you don't get someone else,' flounces Crispin. 'Victor Mature, for instance.'

'He wanted luncheon vouchers,' says my prospective employer acidly. 'Now, concentrate on the performance you're being paid to give.'

'I don't know how you expect anyone to say these lines,' moans Crispin. ' "Man, but it's a really switched-on pad you've here, honey." Good grief, if my old Rada teacher could see me now –'

'Yes, I know, Crispin,' says Justin. 'But the money's good, isn't it? It's better than reading children's stories on the tele. Now, for God's sake, let's have some action!'

'Bunchleys munchy butter-beans just melt in your mouth,' says Crispin for no apparent reason.

'My nipples are going numb,' says Sandra from the bed. 'Jim put that sellotape on too tight.'

'You'll just have to grin and bear it, dear,' says Justin as a groan goes up from the camera crew. 'O.K. Let's get this bleeding scene in the can.'

'Quiet, please!'

'Scene one hundred and forty two – Take three.'

'Mind Sandra when you use that clapper board.'

'Shut up!'

'See nipples and die.'

'Shut up!'

Sandra stands by the bed and Crispin adjusts his hairpiece and squares his shoulders – well, oblongs them really. They are not wide enough to square.

'Man, but it's a really switched-on pad you've got here, honey.'

'You like it, do you?'

'Like it. I love it.'

'That chest for instance.' Mac's camera is honing in on Sandra's boobs.

'You like my chest?'

'I love your chest. There's one thing, though.'

'What's that?'

'I think it needs a coat of paint.'

'You want to paint my chest?'

'Yes. I'll go and get my brush.'

'All right, I'll get it ready for you.' As Crispin turns his back Sandra shrugs off her negligee and Mac's camera lens nearly caps the tips of her titties. Sandra lies down on the bed and Crispin comes into camera holding a brush and a can of paint.'

'O.K., Crispin,' coaches Justin. 'Register surprise. Good. Now Sandra, take his paintbrush. Bite it. Good. That's lovely. Beautiful. Hold it there for a couple of secs. Lovely. Now down. Super. Crispin, get on top of her. Not too fast! Don't leave Mac behind. Right, now reach for the paintbrush, Crispin. Both your hands on it. On the paintbrush, Crispin!! Lovely. That's beautiful. Kiss Down, down, down. And paintbrush into the tin. Lovely! Right, cut. That was beautiful. We'll do one more to be on the safe side but we'll certainly print that one. What do you want?' Justin has suddenly become aware that I am standing by his side.

'Miss Mealie sent me. She said you needed a window cleaner. I spoke to your office this morning.'

'Your what?' says Mac.

'Shut up,' says Justin and turns back to me. 'How is the winsome slut. Still fucking everything that moves?'

'Nearly everything,' I say resentfully.

'You're the fellow who was in the paper today, aren't you?' says Mac who has been peering at me closely. 'Did you see it, Justin?'

'I only read the *Financial Times*,' says Justin coolly. 'What were you doing in the papers?'

'Miss Mealie cooked up some publicity gimmick which had me prancing about in the altogether.'

'You've got the right pedigree for this caper, then. Have you got a card?'

I dive into my breast pocket and retrieve the card Miss Mealie has given me.

'No, no, dear boy. That's my card, isn't it? I mean a union card?'

'No.'

'My God. Did you hear that, Mac? You're not allowed to buy a copy of the ABC Film Review without a union card.' He looks round the set. 'If these people knew you weren't a card holder, they'd be out of that door like lemmings.'

'I'm sorry. Where do I get one?'

'You can't get one unless you're an actor.'

'But I can't be an actor unless I've got one.'

'Exactly. Clever, isn't it? Don't worry. We'll get you one.'

'What do you want me to do?'

'Nothing at the moment. I want to use you for some scene-setting stuff, probably tomorrow. You know, shining up ladders. Standing on window ledges. That kind of thing. All exterior shots.'

'Don't I have to say anything?'

'No, but don't worry. It's degrading to have to speak on this kind of film, isn't it, Crispin?'

Crispin shudders and continues to pat his hair.

'Completely unnecessary, too. We like to keep the actor's lips moving to give the impression that they're alive but apart from that it's busts, bottoms and bums all the way. Sandra's mammaries are the language our audience understands.'

'Couple of flashes from Sandra and the centre of Singapore is ablaze with burning taxis,' agrees Mac.

'A lot of your stuff goes abroad, does it?' I ask.

'We wouldn't be in business without our export market. That's another reason why we play down the dialogue. If you're trying to flog a movie everywhere from Bangkok to Budleigh Salterton, you've got to keep it simple. You noticed the international flavour we injected into the piece you saw?'

'Yes,' I say, 'very sophisticated.'

'Don't knock it. That's what the audience wants. They don't listen to the words.'

'Did you say we were going to do another take of this scene?' says Crispin petulantly. 'I'm not wed to my craft, you know.'

'Crispin is what they call an old pro,' explains Justin. 'He came to us from Children's Hour via the West London Magistrates Court.'

I watch them do the scene again and it occurs to me how blasé everyone is. There is lovely Sandra revealing her all and most of the blokes on the set are playing cards or kipping. Even Sandra herself calmly chucks aside her copy of *The Lady* before getting on with it. I suppose the glamour must wear off after a while. Luckily the blood is still running dangerously hot through my veins and when Justin announces that shooting is over for the day I am swift to offer Big S. her robe.

'Ta, love,' she says. 'Did you say you were a window cleaner?'

'I used to be.'

'That's a pity. I hoped I could press you into service. I can't get anyone to come near me.'

'You amaze me,' I husk. 'Tell you what: I'm not doing very much at the moment. Why don't I give your windows a quick once over?'

All the time I am talking to her I cannot take my eyes off her knockers and she pulls her robe across her chest protectively.

'You're sure it's no trouble?'

'None at all.'

'All right. I won't be long.'

When Sandra comes out of the dressing room she leads the way to the car park and steers me towards a bubble car, the shape of which is a perfect match for her own best feature.

'It's very economical for hopping about in,' she says. 'As long as you don't mind a bit of a crush.' She reaches across to shut the door and for a second I feel as if I'm bringing in the melon harvest. 'Snug, isn't it?'

'Very. Tell me, how many films have you made?' I say, demonstrating that gift for conversation that has made me the darling of my mum's Tupperware parties.

'I've no idea. About twenty, I think.'

'I don't even know your full name.'

'At the moment it's Sandra Virgin. I've had about six. Paula Rental, Dreft Sunsilk –'

'Dreft Sunsilk?'

'Yes. My manager had the idea of getting manufacturers to sponsor me. It never caught on though. It's a cute name, don't you think?'

'Very. Why do they keep changing them?'

'They change them every time they re-launch me. I think they've stopped now. I hope so. I get fed up with it. They've even done a feature on the number of times I've been launched.'

'What's your favourite name?'

'Sandra Finch. That's my real name.'

'Finch! It's not really big enough, is it?'

'That's what they kept saying. They'd have liked to have called me Sandra Jumbotits, or something.'

'Who's they?'

'I have an agent and Justin has taken a big interest in my career.'

'He seems to know what he's doing.'

'Oh, he's brilliant. Very clever. He went to Oxford, you know. The University.'

'I have heard of it.'

'Yes. Since he set up Trion we haven't looked back.

43

He's marvellous at finding out what people want and giving it to them.'

'I don't think I've ever seen any of his films.'

'Well, you wouldn't. Most of them go abroad. They do show in the West End though. Underwater Sex was on at the Burlington for months.' Now she mentions it, I do remember a poster saying: 'Their love was so hot even the Adriatic could not put it out.'

'You filmed that on location did you?'

'On location! You must be joking. We shot it all in a tank in five days. I got a terrible cold. It was awful having to hold your breath down there. And all those octopuses! It was disgusting the things they got up to. Squirting muck everywhere.'

'So you do everything in a studio?'

'In a room if possible. Justin is the king of the low budget production. He makes Andy Warhol seem like Cecil B. de Mille.'

'They're all sex pictures?'

'Not completely. I mean, there are sex pictures and sex pictures. Justin was the first producer to hit on the idea of the instructional sex film that demonstrates how to do it. It's wonderful, because you don't need any dialogue and, if it's instructional it can't be dirty. Professor Blumsticker reads his casebook and we do a fade from his surgery to the bedroom, with his voice over.'

'His voice over what?'

'Over the action on the screen. My, my, you don't know much about it, do you? Quite the little greenhorn.'

Not so much of the 'little' or the 'green', I think to myself but I don't say anything. It is not in my nature to give offence to the owner of such a magnificent pair of knockers.

When we get to Sandra's house I see that it is one of those old Victorian jobs which has more windows than a fish has scales. Sandra reads my expression.

'I'm afraid you've got your work cut out,' she says. "You'd better tell me what you'd like and I'll see if I can accommodate you.' She raises an eyebrow and winks at me.

'In the way of equipment, of course. I'm sorry, but when you've been in as many of Justin's films as I have everything sounds like a double-entendre.' She takes a deep breath and half the oxygen in the car disappears. I'm not kidding, this lady's breathing equipment is really constructed on the grand scale.

'I take it you're married?' I say as we crunch across the gravel.

'Married and separated.'

'Oh dear. You live here all by yourself do you?' It is difficult to keep a note of satisfaction out of my evil little voice.

'Yes, except for Fido.' We are approaching the front door as she speaks and I can see the outline of something pressing against the frosted glass. 'Poor dear. I have to leave him at home and he misses me dreadfully.' I smile sympathetically and think what a lot of noise little Fido can make. Little Fido! By the cringe, but I was never so mistaken about the size of anything since I caught a glimpse of Tiny Trotter's chopper when we changed in the same cubicle at Tooting Bec Baths. Fido makes the Hound of the Baskervilles seem like Sooty's kid sister. He comes through the door like an express train and has to stoop to rest his front paws on Sandra's shoulders.

'There, there boysie,' she says. 'Did naughty mumsie leave her favourite doggy alone all day? Wicked mumsie!' The brute licks her face in a way that suggests a great future stripping paintwork and then looks at me and yawns. At least, I hope it yawns. Whatever it does I see enough big yellow teeth to kit out a couple of sharks.

'I think he's hungry,' says Sandra.

'You leave him plenty of food, I suppose?' I croak as Fido starts sniffing one of my legs. 'I wouldn't like him to think I was some kind of cocktail snack.'

'Heel, Fido!' says Sandra firmly. 'Don't do that to Mr. Lea, it's not nice. Mumsie will give you your din-dins right away.'

I follow Sandra through to the kitchen and watch fascinated as Fido folds his chops around what looks like half a sheep. He adjusts his molars and engages full crunch in a way that convinces me he could bite a hole in the side of a battleship.

'He's lovely, isn't he?' says Sandra, like she was peering into a cot full of first-born.

'Yeah. Quite a character,' I say. 'Now, have you got a bucket and some old rags? It'll be very handy, this. Good practice for the shooting tomorrow.'

Sandra kits me out and I leave her preparing a fry-up. 'Got to feed the inner woman,' she observes. I am not surprised to learn that there is more than one in there.

I get a ladder from the garage and notice a very elegant old banger standing on blocks.

'That's Henry's,' says Sandra when I ask her about it later. 'He used to spend hours tinkering with it. I made some for you. Is that all right?' She is referring to a plateful of sausages, kidneys and bacon and that is definitely all right. 'I always get ravenous when I'm on the set,' she continues. 'It's funny really because I don't use up a lot of energy.'

'Don't you have to watch your figure?' I ask.

'I've got enough people doing that for me,' says witty Sandra. 'That's one of the reasons my old man pushed off. That and the fact that I was making twice as much money as he was. I should have told him I suppose.'

'You mean he didn't know the kind of films you were acting in?'

'Not really, no. Well, he knew the kind of films, but he didn't know the parts I was playing. You see I started off as an extra and then I got noticed.'

'I'm not surprised,' I say, watching her bristols bobbing up and down behind the tea pot. 'You aren't a serious threat to Twiggy are you?'

'Justin noticed my potential and gave me a small part in "Sex in the Suburbs".'

'A small big part,' I say. 'I'm afraid I missed that one.'

'Henry caught up with me in "Titty, Titty, Gang Bang". I don't know why he kicked up so much fuss because he sneaked off to see it without me knowing. He didn't realise I was in it, you see. Thought he was going to get a crafty thrill on the side. Fido!! Stop doing that! He's taken a fancy to you, hasn't he?' Fido is also trying to get a crafty thrill on the side. 'I tried to tell him that he was being ridiculous but it didn't do any good. He said he could never feel the same about me again. I said what's the difference between watching sexy films and appearing in them? But he could never see that. Then one of his friends saw me and that was it. He couldn't bear the thought of all his mates "lapping me up", as he put it.'

I nod in agreement but secretly I have more than a little sympathy for Henry. I mean, I would not care for the thought of my old lady frisking about in the altogether while a cinema full of dirty old geezers fidgeted easily with the fronts of their plastic macs.

'It must have been a bit difficult with you bringing in more money than him. I can sympathise there,' I say, trying not to be too much of a fink to my principles.

'I don't see the difference it makes. Ooh, Fido! You are a naughty boy, aren't you? Leave Mr. Lea alone. He wants affection you see.'

'He's quite good at dishing it out too, isn't he?' I say trying to close my legs and push Fido's calf head away. Fido flashes his teeth at me again and I do not think he is practising a friendly grin.

'You're a marvellous cook,' I say. 'This is great.'

'Go on with you. That's just a fry-up. Anybody could do that.'

'My mum couldn't,' I say with feeling. 'She fries bread without using a pan. She thinks Cordon Bleu is a French swear word.'

'Not taken the plunge then?' says Sandra. 'Still living at home?'

'Yes, and I'm not married. And most of the work I've been doing lately has taken me round the country so it hasn't been worth looking for a flat.'

'I need a lodger in this place, really,' says Sandra, avoiding my eye. 'It's ridiculous, Fido and me sharing all this.'

'Yes. A feller would be handy sometimes, too, wouldn't

he? I mean –' I say hurriedly,' – in case you had burglars or wanted a fuse mended.'

'That as well,' smiles Sandra readjusting the tea cosy over the pot in a way that for some reason I find dead sexy. 'Have you finished?'

'Yes. You should be able to see what's happening outside now.' It's not exactly vintage Noel Coward is it? If only there was some subtle way of suggesting that a spot of the other would be much appreciated, apart from shoving my hand up her knicks. Fido would probably have it off faster than you can say plastic surgery – have my arm off, I mean.

Sandra is showing no signs of eagerness to conduct me to the door and is in the process of refilling our cups.

'Didn't take you long did it?'

'It's a knack,' I say modestly. 'What did your old man do?'

'He's a butcher. It came in very handy for feeding Fido.' I look across to where the dirty great brute is crunching up bones, and nod slowly. I hope Sandra's better half is not the resentful type. 'He wanted to take Fido with him but I put my foot down. It suddenly came to me that I preferred the dog to him. You know what I mean?'

'I think so,' I say, wondering what Clement Freud would make of it all. I never reckon dogs much myself so it is difficult for me to be enthusiastic. Give me a budgerigar every time. You don't have to take them for walks and they are much easier to clean up after.

'Are you serious about taking in lodgers?' I say deciding that the time has come to try and bring a little flow and movement into our relationship. 'You have got a lot of bedrooms haven't you? I noticed them while I was doing the windows.'

'Six,' says Sandra proudly. 'The house used to belong to Henry's father. He was quite a prosperous man in his way. There's one end of the house completely empty at the moment. I'm very glad to have Fido here to look after me sometimes.'

'Yes. It must get a bit spooky, I suppose.'

'Would you be interested in having a look round? I wasn't quite certain whether you were looking for something?'

'I haven't quite made up my mind yet,' I drag my eyes off her caged boobs and try and calm myself with a sip of tea. It is strange but when they are locked up I find them much more compelling than when they had the freedom of the film set. Like Christmas presents. The moment you start getting the wrapping paper off, the excitement begins to disappear.

'Are you ready then?'

I gulp down the rest of my tea and scramble to my feet.

'You stay there, Fido. We don't need you.' Sandra points a stern finger at her pooch and the brute slouches over to a basket that looks more like one of those things ancient Britons used to go fishing in. She is dead right. We do not want Fido padding round after us.

'You could have your own key, of course,' says Sandra helpfully. 'Come and go as you please.'

'Sounds very nice,' I say, running my fingers lightly over the large wooden ball at the bottom of the bannisters.

'Have to mind that when you slide down,' says Sandra. I favour her with a light laugh and we ascend to the first floor.

'There's a room at the end of the corridor which might suit you.'

Before we get to it I pause outside a half open door and take a gander at what surely must be the nuptial couch.

'Big bed,' I say trying not to load the words with too much significance.

'I like a bit of room. Don't want to keep bumping into people do you? I'm a restless sleeper.'

I can imagine. Her and those enormous knockers thrashing from side to side all night. You would need extra large sheets.

'I wouldn't know,' I say innocently, giving her the

49

opportunity to say that she bets I do, which she does not take.

'You'd have your own bathroom,' she says, throwing open a door. 'How does that grab you?'

'Marvellous. Dad never got around to applying for the grant.'

'You mean, you don't have a bath at home?'

'Don't worry about it. I know how they work. That thing sticking out of the wall is a foot bath, isn't it?'

'Are you serious?'

'Very. I got my foot stuck round the bend once. Most uncomfortable, it was.'

'You're having me on,' Sandra gives me a big nudge in the ribs which I do not take exception to. Once birds start prodding and touching you then a spot of oggins is seldom as far away as the final payment on your colour tele. 'I like a man with a sense of humour. Henry was very morose. That's the nice thing about the film business. We have a lot of laughs. Most of us have been together for quite some time now and there's a very happy atmosphere on the set.'

'I must have hit you on a bad day.'

'Yes. It was a bit quiet this afternoon. It's Crispin you see. That's not really his line. Well, you can tell, can't you? Our regular man is down with a cold.'

'Who's that?'

'Glint Thrust. Ah, here we are.' Sandra opens a door and I find myself looking into a small room wearing very bright flower-patterned wallpaper.

'Boy! It's instant sunshine, isn't it?'

'It does cheer it up, doesn't it? The room is a tiny bit dark, you see. I thought it needed a splash of colour.'

'Yeah. It got it, didn't it? All over the ceiling too.'

'I'm glad you like it.' Sandra is jumping the gun because I do not like it one little bit, but I am too good-mannered to say so.

'What's the bed like?'

Sandra extends a 'be my guest' hand and I prod the bed

gingerly. 'Get on it if you like. Have a bounce. It won't collapse.'

'How do you know?'

Sandra shudders. 'Never you mind that.'

'Who's this bloke. Glint Lust?'

'Glint Thrust. Why did you suddenly mention him?'

'It struck me as being a funny name.'

'Not as funny as Trevor Hepplethwaite. That was his real name.'

'Did he come here?' I say, noticing that Sandra has registered considerable signs of discomfiture since I mentioned his name.

'You ask too many questions.' She turns and goes out of the room. Oh dear, this is not going at all well. How am I going to achieve the breakthrough that will lock lovely Sandra and myself in sexual congress? I clamber onto the bed and contemplate an attack of cramp but this seems a trifle laboured.

'Well?' Sandra is standing in the doorway.

'Very nice. I like a hard mattress.'

'Hard mattress? You must be joking. It's like puff pastry, this one.' She sits down on the edge of the bed and my pulse quickens.

'You're better equipped to find things soft,' I say. 'I don't carry your protection.'

'Go on with you. There's nothing wrong with that mattress. Now, are you going to get up?'

This is what I believe they call a moot point and at the present rate of progress the answer is probably 'no'.

'It's very comfortable here,' I say. 'I wasn't complaining about the mattress.' Sandra attempts to rise but I hold her hand. 'Don't go,' I say.

'Why not?' I was afraid she might say that and I have very few convincing arguments to restrain her.

'Because I like looking at you.'

'You can look at me standing up. Come on.'

'Come to bed with me, Sandra.' I don't usually like coming right out with it but in my present situation I cannot think of anything else to do. Once we are outside

51

the room I will never have such a good chance again. Also, I feel at an advantage lying down. It is like when you are in hospital. All the people standing round the bed look so uncomfortable.

'You've got a cheek. I hardly know you.'

This is not a totally unexpected response and I move to counter it. 'It's the same for me. I hardly know you either, but I am prepared to give you a chance. I trust the feeling that drew me to you. It doesn't matter how long you've known a person, it matters whether you feel anything.'

'But supposing I don't feel anything?'

'I feel enough for both of us.'

'You're mad. I didn't know you existed until half past five this afternoon and now you're talking about sleeping with me.'

'I never mentioned sleep. Sandra, listen. It makes such good sense. You say you don't know me. What better way to get acquainted? Get all the sexual tension out of the air. If I move in here, imagine what it could be like if I kept bumping into you coming out of the bathroom? You'd start fretting about it. Wonder if I was doing it on purpose. Now if we go to bed with each other straight away we'll get rid of all the sexual tension that could haunt our relationship. There won't be anything to get worked up about.'

'But I like sexual tension.'

'Not all the sexual tension,' I say hurriedly, 'just the damaging bit. I want to earth the fuse, not stop paying the electricity bill. I must be honest with you, Sandra. You're so beautiful that I don't think I could stay near you if I thought I was never going to make love to you.' I can see that this goes down better than a buttered marshmallow and I squeeze Sandra's hand passionately and pull her towards me.

'I don't believe a word of it,' she says.

'Oh, Sandra.'

'Load of stuff and nonsense.'

'Sandra!' My cry is like that of a small wild animal in pain.

'Just this once then,' Sandra pushes the door shut behind her and stands up. 'But don't think you're fooling me. I'm probably being very stupid.'

I defeat an impulse to leap off the bed and start tearing my clothes off and lean back with my hands behind my head while I let my eyes roam up and down her roller-coaster body.

'Fantastic,' I breathe.

'I'm human, you see,' says Sandra almost bitterly as she fiddles behind her back for the hook on her bra. 'I have a libido too.'

I imagine she is talking about the thing in the bathroom but who wants to wash their feet at a moment like this?

'Allow me,' I say. 'I'd hate you to strain yourself.' I get off the bed and unclip her bra. By the cringe, but that thing is under some tension. When I release the catch I am darn nearly jerked over her shoulder by the weight of her bristols. She wriggles round and I find that by craning my neck I can get close enough to kiss her. She is very good at this and when her tongue goes into action I know how a foxglove must feel when it is being given the once over by a pollen-crazy bee. My hands have just gone to launch on a haunch when my concentration is shattered by the sound of a heavy body battering against the bedroom door. Being less than a complete stranger to this kind of situation, my first reaction is one of blind, stumbling panic. Sandra's husband, his striped apron flecked with blood, is at this moment pulling his straw hat over his eyes and swinging back his cleaver for its first appointment with my nut.

'You'd better let him in,' says Sandra, disentangling herself from my mouth. 'He'll scratch the door down if you don't.'

My mind clears and I realise she is talking about the nauseous Fido.

'Do I have to?' I whine.

'He has been alone all day, poor pet, and he hates being left out of anything,' says Sandra breezily. 'Let him in. We won't get any peace if you don't.'

She may have a point there. The noise of scratching from outside the door suggests that Fido is holding an electric fan against it.

I turn the handle and my wrist is darn near broken as our four-legged friend bounds into the room. What with Sandra's knockers, the technicolor wallpaper and Fido, there is precious little space left for me. Nevertheless, I intend to make the most of it.

'Down, boy!' Sandra is talking to Fido and the brute retires to a corner and starts whacking the wall with its tail. 'Now, where were we? U-u-u-u-m . . .' She leans across her enormous bristols and settles greedily onto my mouth. She is wearing a long cotton skirt fastened loosely at the waist, as I find out when I send my fingers into action. I never stood a chance of getting one of those scout badges for tying knots – but untying them! Her own pinkies are not qualifying for unemployment benefit and she quickly gets to work on the buttons that litter the front of my Fort Laramie Frontier Cords. These open up for pleasure and necessity by means of a trapdoor of material covering the area of my crutch and it does not take Sandra long to get to the hang of how this works.

'Nice trousers,' she says as we separate for a spot of breathing. She is not the only one to be attracted by them. As they sink gracefully to take up their natural position on the floor, Fido bounds forward and playfully rips them from my person like they are an unwanted piece of sticking plaster.

'Fido! Bad boy! Mumsie is going to be angry with you!' Dadsie is already very angry and I am thinking what a nice warm rug the perishing pooch would make if one had an elephant gun handy. Artists like myself are easily put off their stroke by such interruptions. Not so Sandra. Her stroke is faultless and speedily brings me back to an awareness of the job in hand. Her skirt is soon at floor level and her cotton-picking fingers have reduced me to the state in which dad first expressed concern about my resemblance to the coalman, e.g. one of becoming nudity.

For late-comers, the score is, Timmy: naked; Sandra: panties and tights with off the shoulder blouse nearly off the shoulder. I am about to equal things up when Sandra suddenly grips me rather tighter than has been her wont.

'Did you hear something?' she hisses.

'Only Fido chewing up one of my shoes.'

'No, something downstairs.'

'Your husband?!' Those unpleasant stabbing pains have started again.

'I don't know. You'd better go and look.'

'Me! Why me? Why not send Fido?'

'Fido's a terrible coward. He wouldn't hurt a fly, really. You're not afraid, are you?'

'No. But –'

'Go on. I'm scared. There have been a lot of burglaries around here lately.'

'I'm not worried about burglars. Supposing it's your husband?'

'It can't be. I've just remembered. He's in Frankfurt at the moment, at a convention. Go on. Hurry up. Then you can come back to me.' She gives a delicious little wriggle that makes it difficult for me to consider refusing her anything. 'Go on.' She puckers her lips and runs her fingers lightly along my Action Man kit.

'All right,' I say. 'But I'm not going to be long.'

'Oh, I don't know. You're not doing badly.' I ignore that and scamper out into the corridor. The clocks have gone back and it is distinctly dark outside. Dark and foggy. I can see the glow of a street lamp and the outline of trees but precious little else. I would like to turn a few lights on but in my present state of undress it does not seem like a very good idea. I stand still for a couple of minutes but can hear nothing. Good. Sandra was obviously mistaken. I am on the point of returning to the bedroom when there is a sound from downstairs. At least I think it is downstairs. It may have come from outside in the street. Knickers! I suppose I had better go and have a look. If only I wasn't so brave and noble. I get to the top of the stairs and listen again. Nothing. There is a light switch by my hand and, since I am hidden from outside view, I flick it on, hoping that any intruders will take the hint and make a run for it. Not a sausage. My reservoir of courage has practically dried up, but I slink downstairs keeping closer to the wall than the wallpaper. The hall is bathed in light and seems empty. Of course it seems empty! But any berk who has ever seen an Alfred Hitchcock movie knows that the mad butcher of Boreham Wood is waiting behind the hallstand with his chopper in his hands. This is virtually all I have to defend myself with and the thought encourages me to indulge in another long spell of listening. All seems well, but, wait! Looking towards the frosted glass front door I think I catch a glimpse of something moving outside. What can it be? A prowler? A peeping Tom? My imagination? The outline of my body will be seen through the glass if I walk to the door so I decide to approach it on all fours and peer through the letter-box which is situated a little above ground level. In that manner I can check that everything is alright and then return to lovely, curvy Sandra. What a little pleasure factory she promises to be. I am practically hugging myself at the thought of it as I sink to ground level and start crawling across the hall carpet. I don't know if you have ever tried crawling with your hampton at the stand-by, but it is not an experience I would recommend. It is draughty too. All in all I am glad when I have covered the fifteen feet that separates me from the letter-box. Pausing to listen once more, I pull back the flap and peer outside. Two milk bottles, some leaves, a garden – O-O-O-O-O-W!!

When Sandra eventually comes down it is to find me with my head and shoulders stuck through the frosted glass panel of the front door just above the letter-box.

'I've rung for the police,' she squeals. 'Are you alright? Whatever happened?'

My voice has a certain world-weary quality as I withdraw my body and start to shake pieces of broken glass out of my hair.

'Bleeding Fido came up behind me and started licking my balls,' I tell her.

CHAPTER FOUR

'O.K., Timmy, you can put your plasters back on now. We've got all we want.'

It is the day after my encounter with Sandra's front door and I have just finished a tiring stint before the cameras. As far as I can make out I am Crispin's stand-in which does not fill me with great enthusiasm, as I have to remove all the sticking plasters which are holding my face together.

'Can't take any chances,' says Mac, the cameraman, 'although I don't reckon they'll show, up there.'

'Up there' turns out to be a number of terrifyingly high window ledges on which I am called upon to disport myself while Justin collects the outside shots that he requires to string together the twenty-seven different sexual episodes in the film.

'First four films we made, we never went outside the studio once, did we, Mac?' says Justin breezily.

'We only went inside the studio twice,' says Mac. 'The first three were shot in that girl's flat. You know, the one you fixed up with that apartment in Tangiers. Whatever happened –?'

'Yes, yes,' says Justin, running his fingers through his shoulder-length hair. 'No need to tell everybody about my munificence. They'll all want flats, won't they? I often hear from Sonia. She's having a lovely time.' He turns to me. 'Splendid performance, Timothy, absolutely splendid. I'm certain you have a talent we could exploit.'

'He'll exploit it, all right,' muttered Mac. 'There's no doubt about that.'

'Fail not to record that I have some of the sharpest ears in the business, sweetheart,' murmurs Justin in a chilling whisper, 'and that people who take the mickey make me sickey.'

'No offence,' says Mac quickly. 'Just my little joke.'

'Make them larger or not at all,' warns Justin. 'Now, Timothy, as I was saying, before I was so crudely interrupted, I think that with your physique and appearance you could be a considerable asset to Trion Productions. You're cast in the same mould as Glint Thrust and it would do him good to know that there was some competition breathing down his neck.'

I am so excited that I can hardly speak. One day in the studio and I am already on the threshold of stardom!

'Where is Mr. Thrust?' I ask.

Mac looks at Justin who pauses for a minute and then permits himself a strained smile. 'He's been ill,' he says. 'Picked up an infection. We thought it best to nip it in the bud.'

'He's accident-prone,' says Mac.

Justin shoots his colleague a warning glance and puts an arm round my shoulder.

'I'm trying to get something big off the ground. If it comes off then we must talk again. I take it you are interested?'

'Oh yes, Mr. Tymely.'

'Call me Justin. We're all one big happy family here, aren't we, Mac?'

'Yes, sir,' says Mac, touching his forelock.

Sandra has not been involved in any of the outdoor shooting and I have not seen her since we rummaged through the first-aid box together. Apart from the shaking-up I received, the sight of my phizog covered in bits of plaster does little to recapture the flavour of our earlier pre-grind touch-up and I eventually venture home by means of the Northern Line without suffering any loss of weight in the y-front area.

Returning to Scraggs Lane after the exterior shooting, I am surprised to find brother-in-law Sidney stuck into a cup of cha in the kitchen. There is a satisfied expression on his mush not dissimilar to that worn by cats with canary feathers sticking out of the corners of their cake-holes.

'Hello, Timmy,' he says. 'Mum tells me you've become a

59

bleeding film star. Can you get me lined up with a bit of crumpet?'

'You do all right for yourself, Sidney,' I tell him. 'How's the Cromby?'

'Same as usual. Miss Ruperts had one of her turns and came down to dinner stark naked. I didn't see it myself but I hear it was a disgusting eyeful.'

'Sounds very nasty, Sid. How are the vacuum cleaners?'

Sidney pushes his teacup away from him and looks at me thoughtfully. 'Funny you should mention that, Timmo.'

'I thought you might say that.'

'There was an accident.'

'No.'

'Yes. Most unfortunate.'

'Let me guess. Not a fire by any chance?'

Sidney extends his arms and sighs deeply. 'I know just what you're thinking – but you're wrong. I admit it did flash across my mind to set fire to the whole bleeding lot of them and collect the insurance. But, when it came to the pinch – well, you know me. Do you think I could do it?'

'Sidney. This is probably going to come as a big surprise to you but, in a word: yes. Not only that but I think you could probably claim for the matches as a tax deduction.'

Sidney closes his eyes and adopts an expression of anguish the like of which I have not seen since they last showed 'On the Waterfront' on the tele.

'Oh, Timmo, Timmo. How can you say that. I know we've had our ups and downs but if I can't rely on you to believe me, who can I rely on?'

I stare at Sidney blankly because, for the life of me, I cannot think of anyone. Maybe he shares my uncertainty because he continues without waiting for an answer: 'Fireworks, Timothy. Fireworks. That's what did it. You may recall that Guy Fawkes Day has just passed?'

'I do recall that, Sidney.'

'A stray rocket through one of the windows.'

More like a two-inch mortar shell, I think to myself, but I remain silent.

'Couldn't the fire brigade do anything?'

'They were all out on calls at the time.'

'What a coincidence.'

'Are you trying to suggest something?'

'No, Sid. I was just wondering what that piece of sticking plaster was doing round your index finger.'

'If you're suggesting –'

'That you rang in a whole lot of false alarms to keep the firemen busy while the warehouse burned down? Sidney! You know me better than that.'

'It was an accident, so help me!'

'Sid, it doesn't matter if I believe you. It's the insurance company that counts. I take it from the happy expression that was on your mug when I came through the door that they have coughed up?'

'Justice has been done,' says Sid grandly.

'So you're in the ackers again?'

'I have recouped my loss. Yes.'

'And no sign of Ishowi.'

Sidney's expression hardens. 'No! Perishing little nip bastard! I wish he'd gone up with the cleaners.'

'Sidney! Really. That's no way to talk of an ex-colleague. You used to think very highly of him.'

'Come off it! You can't think highly of someone who only stands four-foot-six off the bleeding ground!'

Sidney is definitely one to bear a grudge and there is obviously very little chance of him being invited to take the chair at the next meeting of the Anglo-Nippon Friendship Society. 'I should have remembered what they did in the war,' he says bitterly. 'Your father warned me. It's the only good bit of advice the bleeding old git has ever given me.'

Any love lost between Sid and my dad could be found wedged in the eye of a small needle and to remind me of this fact, Father Lea's weary frame struggles into the kitchen and slumps into the only vacant chair.

'Hello,' he says, nodding at me and then at mum.

'Bleeding Ramon Navarro's back with us, I see. Discussing a documentary on work-shy spongers, are you?'

'If we were, you'd be a dead cert for the leading role, dad,' says Sid.

'Don't you "dad" me. I never had no part in you!'

'I should hope not. What a disgusting thing to say!'

'Talk about work. You don't know what it means. I've been slaving away down there since nine o'clock. Not a drop of food nor drink has passed my lips since I had a cup of tea this morning before you lot were up.'

'That pong of beer is your deodorant, I suppose?' I venture.

'Deodorant?' says Sid. 'He can't use one. When it gets a whiff of his armpits, that white stick thing shrinks back up the tube and won't come down again.'

'That's marvellous, isn't it?' explodes dad. 'Decent working-class man slaves away all day and then comes back to be revealed in his own home. No wonder this bleeding country is going to the dogs. Any greedy, work-shy little basket can fiddle his way into a fortune while decent ordinary people have to scrimp and save to find two pennies to rub together.

'You scrimped and saved enough to buy a colour tele, didn't you?'

'Blimey! I'm entitled to a little pleasure, aren't I? I can't afford to go out. What do you expect me to do? Watch the pattern on the wallpaper?'

'You go out to the boozer,' says mum.

'That's fantastic, that is! Now you turn on me. I only got that colour tele because I thought it would give you some pleasure.

'You only got it because my Premium Bond came up,' says mum.

'That only paid for the deposit!' bellows dad. 'Who's looking after the instalments, then? You tell me that. I don't know why I go on, I really don't.'

'I don't know why you go on, either,' says Sid. 'Why don't you belt up or drop dead or something?'

The situation is quivering on the brink of unpleasantness but luckily Rosie chooses that moment to bring Jason back from the Natural History Museum, where apparently he tried to nick half a Brontosaurus, and mum dishes up supper. Delicious tangy, Coddyburgers, fried a tempting golden black in rich diesel oil.

'Don't you reckon your frying pan needs an oil change?' says Sid.

'Eat them up, dear,' says mum good-humouredly. 'They're very good for you. It says "a dish fit for a king" on the packet.'

'More like "a dish fit for aching,"' mutters Sidney. He should worry. I am so much in favour, now that I am a film actor, that mum gives me the extra portion.

No more is said about Sid collecting the insurance money from the burnt-out warehouse but I recall the subject when I am on the set of 'Up the Ladder, Jack' the following day. Justin has called me in because he thinks that I may be needed for a few interior shots and I hear him talking to Mac about the finance for their next epic.

'You don't know anybody with a few thou to invest in the movie business, do you?' he says to me jokingly. 'Most of my cash is tied up in production work at the moment and I need some liquid funds. The front office pay-out can be very slow sometimes.'

'Very, very slow,' says Mac. Justin glares at him.

I am about to say no, when it suddenly occurs to me that Sidney is in the ackers again. What better way of cementing myself to Justin's bosom than by introducing him to Sid? At the very least the gesture should be appreciated, and if by any chance Sid does lash out some mazuma, Trion Productions can hardly fail but to reward me with a leading role. Also, such an arrangement has the advantage of preventing my natural talents being shackled to Sid. In the past I have been too much under his thumb in our working arrangements.

'Funny you should say that, Mr. Tymely,' I observe. 'My brother-in-law, Sidney Noggett, is in the hotel business and he has a bit of money to invest at the moment. He struck lucky recently.'

While I enjoy my little joke Justin strokes his silk scarf and raises an eyebrow in a gesture which I think is intended to suggest casual interest.

'Really? I'd like to meet your brother-in-law some time. Is he in town?'

'He is at the moment. Usually he's down at Hoverton where the hotel is.'

'Interesting. Perhaps we can arrange lunch sometime.' He turns his attention back to the actors. 'O.K., Crispin, let's do it again. Remember "Oh my God, it's my husband!" – off the bed and into the wardrobe. And do be careful how you close the door this time. We used the last of the sticking plaster on your toupee, remember?'

Justin says no more about Sidney but later on in the afternoon the girl who was being groped when I first arrived at the studio, and is apparently Justin's personal assistant, checks out Sidney's address with me. She is a nice looking bird, that one, always covered in confusion and love bites. I think she must have a very hectic social life.

'Hello, we've never really met,' she gasps, sweeping hair out of her eye. 'Samantha Toots. Call me Sam, everybody does. Justin wanted to know where I could get hold of your brother-in-law.'

I discount some of the more obvious answers to that one and give her the telephone number of the Lea residence in Scraggs Lane. Yes, with little Jason on the verge of becoming an international star, mum and Rosie forced dad into lashing out on what he regards as a vast waste of money. He is double choked when he finds that he gets a set of telephone books free because he has been lovingly cherishing a set of old ones in the hallstand along with his porn collection. These phone books are so ancient the numbers are in roman numerals.

When I get home Sidney is looking well chuffed with himself and in such a situation is seldom slow to impart the reason for his good humour.

'Who's this bird Samantha, then?' he says. 'She sounds a bit of all right.'

'Oh, you mean Sam,' I say. 'We all call her Sam. Yes, she is pretty attractive. Never wears a bra. Looks like she's got a couple of pom-pom hats down the front of her sweater. Why do you ask?'

'She rang me up. Says her boss wants to have lunch with me. You told him about me, did you?'

'Some of the things about you, Sidney. I didn't want to frighten him off.'

'Looking for fresh talent is he?'

Typical of Sidney to imagine that he is about to be discovered. The poor old sod would be pushed to get a walk-on part in 'Creatures the World Forgot'.

'He's looking for finance, Sid. I mentioned that you might be interested in getting into the film business. You said you'd go of course?'

'Oh yeah. Nothing to lose, have I?'

Experience has taught me to pretend that I do not hear questions like that and I leave Sidney thinking a Wills Whiff into a Havana cigar.

Rather late in the day I find that Justin has also invited me to lunch. Sidney has not been swift to inform me of this fact and I think that he has been hoping that I would fix up a day trip to Southend, or some other convenient alternative to cramping his style.

The restaurant selected for our meeting is in Soho and called something like the Trattoria Grotti. I am not very keen on Greek food myself, never having had any, but I can see that Sidney is bubbling with excitement – probably only at the thought of getting some buckshee nosh.

'Looks a nice place, doesn't it?' he says, rubbing his hands together. 'I reckon I'm going to enjoy this.'

'Probably got the cook we had at the Isla de Amori. Do you remember? The only English words he knew were "stomach pump".'

Sidney ignores this and we advance towards the door which is whipped open as if the waiter is trying to snatch it off its hinges.

'Bon Journo Signori!' he trills. 'What service can I perform for you?'

Justin and Mac are sitting in a corner but they are not alone. Sam is with them, looking very dithery and desirable, and there is a pneumatic blonde bird with about half a ton of mascara plastered round her peepers. She looks like something out of 'Antony and Cleopatra meet Tooting Common on Ice'.

'Splendid to meet you, Mr. Noggett,' beams Justin, extending a hand as I stutter an introduction. 'This is my cameraman, Donald McDonald and this is my personal assistant, Samantha Toots and one of the artists we have under contract, Miss Sadie Masoch. You may remember her in our historical romance, "Fanny Mountain"? Sadie! What's the matter?'

The blonde bint has her hand to her mouth and is gawping at Sidney like he has just dropped from the ceiling and landed on eight legs.

'I'm terribly sorry!' she shrieks in a high-pitched theatrical squeal, 'but just for a moment I thought – well. I suppose you must get terribly bored with people saying this, but it really is remarkable.'

'What is?' Sidney is feeling behind his ears for drifts of shaving soap.

'The resemblance!' Sadie looks at Sam who nods vigorously and tries to make a hole in her Ribena at the same time. Justin pats her on the back. 'Paul Newman!'

With those words my heart sinks. There was once a stupid scrubber who told Sid he looked like Paul Newman and the poor twirp went around chewing matchsticks for three months afterwards.

'Oh, that,' Sidney delivers one of his throw-away smiles which he should have thrown away years ago. 'Yes, it can get a little embarrassing sometimes but you learn to live with it. I'm a bit taller than he is.'

'Really? How interesting,' shrills Sadie. 'Well, darlink, you must come and sit next to me and tell me all about it.'

'It's a shame really,' purrs Justin. 'If you didn't have this incredible resemblance to Paul Newman I'd feel like offering you a role as actor rather than financier. Your kind of –' he waves a hand in the air as if hoping to draw down inspiration.

'Caramba?' says Sidney hopefully.

'Charisma, that's right,' says Justin. 'One finds it so rarely these days.'

If Sidney ever became an actor he would never be able to play modest parts, and it is fortunate that a waiter arrives before he can prove it.

'Signor Justin,' he grovels, 'eez lovely to 'ave you 'ere again. May I recommend the Peto di pollo. Delicious. And the artichokes are also very nice.'

He waits expectantly and everybody looks at Sidney.

'Yes,' says Sid finally, having stared blankly at the menu for several minutes. 'That sounds very nice.'

'I adore corciofi,' trills the blonde job. This comes as no surprise to me but I reckon she would do herself a bit of good by being more secretive about it. I can't stand birds that talk dirty. I look at the menu but can only see one word of English.

'Spaghetti,' I say with dignity.

'Certainly, sir. And to follow?'

I look back down the menu but there is definitely nothing there I have ever heard of.

'Just coffee, thanks,' I say.

'Would you like something with the spaghetti?'

'Chips.'

'Splendid, splendid,' says Justin waving the waiter away when everyone has ordered. 'There's so much pretension about eating out, isn't there? I do like to hear people asking for what they want,' he reached behind him and grabs hold of a passing waiter. 'You uncorked the Valpolicella at eleven-fifteen didn't you? Excellent.' He looks at his watch. 'We'll have that later and start with a bottle of Soave. Make sure it's well chilled won't you?'

'Certainly.' The waiter turns to Sidney. 'Aperitif, sir?'

'No thanks. I've still got my own.'

'He's not talking about dentures, you berk!' I tell him. 'He wants to know if you fancy a snort before munching.'

Really! You would hardly credit it, would you? And he is in the business as well. He embarrasses me sometimes, he really does.

'I'll have a Bleeding Maria,' says Sid. I see Justin and Mac exchanging glances but Sadie continues to gaze into Sidney's mug like it is her favourite painting.

'Uncanny,' she says and I have often had the same feeling myself, although for different reasons.

Sid is definitely flummoxed when his artichoke arrives and I watch with interest as he prepares to deal with it. He pauses for a minute and then, obviously deciding that everybody will sus he has never seen one before unless he gets stuck in fast, sprinkles sugar all over the leaves and starts attacking it with a knife and fork. 'I thought it was some kind of melon,' he says to me afterwards.

Sidney is not doing very well and it is Sam who comes to the rescue.

'Can I have a bit?' she says. Sidney has never been known to refuse such a request from a lady and Sam swiftly selects a leaf and sucks the goody from it in the approved fashion, having dunked it in the bowl of vinaigrette provided. Sidney nearly gets it right only he dips his leaves in the finger bowl.

Although most of the conversation at the meal takes the form of Justin rabbiting on about his ideas for a new film and the fantastic amount of cash it is going to make, it is the meal itself I remember most clearly.

For instance, the moment when Sidney sticks his knife into his Peto di pollo and sends a stream of hot butter down the front of Justin's silk shirt. Also the flaming liqueur called Timbuctoo or something like that. We all have one and after it has burned happily for a couple of minutes and the birds have squeaked with ecstasy at the dizzy excitement of it all, Justin blows his out. Sidney blows his out too. Right out of the glass and down the front of Justin's long-suffering shirt.

In the circumstances it is not surprising that Sidney hardly knows whether he is coming or going and appears to be agreeing to every proposition that Justin fires at him. Mac has excused himself earlier and suddenly Justin leaps to his feet and shoots out a hand.

'Splendid, splendid,' he says. 'So glad you could join us. I'll have the papers drawn up and send them round for your signature. I think one day you'll look back on this meal as a milestone.' He should say millstone but we don't know that then. 'Don't disturb yourselves,' he urges as Sid starts to get up. 'You stay and finish your coffee with the girls. I've got to go and do some editing. Beastly nuisance but there it is.' He waves a hand and is gone.

'I'd love a teeny weeny brandy,' says Sadie who is snuggling up so close to Sidney they could be on the same chair.

By the time she has had a couple of largy wargy brandies, it is occurring to me that I am well and truly pissed and that Sam has the most shapely nipples I have seen outside a jar of gherkins. I am also hopelessly in love with her. In the physical sense of the word of course.

'That was lovely,' she says. 'I feel all warm and glowing inside. I don't want to go back to work.'

'Don't go back to work,' I husk. 'Let's go somewhere where we can make love.' It is smashing being pissed because you can say things like that all day without feeling any kind of embarrassment or hang-up. Sam looks me straight in the eyes and puts her hand on mine.

'Oh dear. I'm so weak,' she breathes. 'I just can't help it.'

'You have beautiful thighs – I mean eyes,' I tell her, looking at her tits. Really, I reckon if I don't get my hands on her soon I am going to explode. 'Where can we go?' I murmur.

Sam looks desperate. 'I don't know. Maybe –' She turns to Sadie who is kissing Sidney in a manner that reminds me of a female vulture feeding its young, and gives her a couple of sharp nudges which eventually prise her off Sid's cakehole. They have a little whisper and depart to powder their noses.

Sid winks at me triumphantly. "I reckon we're away here,' he gloats. I am trying to clear up the coffee spilt when Sidney lurched to his feet as the girls left the table, so it takes me a few minutes to answer. 'What are you doing down there?' says Sid sounding worried.

'Trying to get the coffee stains off my jeans. What do you think, you clumsy berk?'

'I thought you were having yourself away for a minute. Couldn't control your excitement.'

'You're pissed, Sid.'

'Yeah. But what about those two, eh? I reckon even you could score there. What a right couple of little darlings. I should have found out about this movie caper before.'

He opens a box of matches and sticks one between his teeth like Paul Newman. He must be pissed because he has two sticking out of his gob already.

'We hopa very much that you enjoy your meal and we hopa very much to see you again.' The Head Waiter is beaming down at Sidney but Sidney does not beam back.

'What's this then?' he says.

'It's the bill, Sidney,' I tell him. 'You must have seen one before somewhere.'

'But I thought those other blokes were paying?'

'I expect they forgot, Sidney. In the film business little sums of money like that are hardly worth considering.'

Sidney looks at the bill and winces. 'Twenty-eight quid! I don't reckon that's inconsiderable. I reckon its bleeding extravagant. That would keep me in grub for a month.'

I have to be careful with Sid because I don't want him getting all narky and backing out of the deal. My whole future depends on it.

'Pay it and forget about it, Sid. It's an investment compared with what you stand to make out of the picture. And think of those birds you're getting chucked in.'

Luckily the girls return at this moment and I see Sidney's glazed eyes get another coating of frost. 'I'll have to write a cheque,' he grumbles.

'Darlinks,' trills Sadie, 'We thought we'd take you to the cinema. I've got a friend at Fantastic Unbelievable

70

Pictures and I've arranged for us to use one of their projection rooms. That's right, isn't it, Samantha?'

'I'm so weak,' says Sam.

The waiter looks from Sid's cheque to the bill.

'Service is not included,' he says reproachfully.

'Oh dear,' says Sid. 'What a pity. I can never work it out in this new decimal money. Have you got a couple of bob on you, Timmo?'

When we get outside I have a nasty feeling that Sid is going to be bankrupted by having to pay for a taxi but fortunately the home of Fantastic Unbelievable Pictures is just round the corner. It is no more exciting than the studios at Sheppertree and once you get past the blurred and bleeding coloured photographs of some of F.U.P.'s latest epics: 'Revenge of the Creeping Horror', 'They Came in Outer Space', 'Orgy and Bess', it is like any office building.

Sam leads the way down a long, dark corridor and sticks her head round the door of a small office.

'Hello, Trevor,' she says. 'I rang through about that new Arty Spangler movie. Can you put it up for us?'

Would that she would ask me the same question but I can wait. The next door leads into the projection room which is about twenty foot square with thick pile carpets and three tiers of armchair-type seats. There is a small panel of glass behind the seats through which the film can be shown and, of course, a screen.

'Cosy,' says Sidney, winking at me again. 'Very cosy. Right-O, darling? Let's grab a slice of the back row.' He leads Sadie up underneath the projection box and they sink into the armchairs like a couple of pebbles into warm toffee.

'Oh dear,' sighs Sam. 'I just don't seem to be able to control myself.'

'I know exactly how you feel,' I murmur, drawing her down into the front row as the lights dim.

I do not remember very much about the film except the first few minutes which seem to be taking place in a junk yard with a lot of naked chicks and fellows rolling about starkers in the rubbish. There is a good deal of moaning and groaning but I am not certain whether this is coming from the screen or the back row. I look round once and all I can see is one of Sadie's feet hooked over the seat. Sid does not waste much time at the flicks as any of the usherettes at the Odeon, Balham will tell you. When you have seen him in action it comes as no surprise that he can hardly remember a thing about any of the pictures he has paid to see. He saw 'Gigi' three times and still came out thinking it was about horse-racing.

Not that I am concentrating on Sidney's performance. Oh dear me, no! Once Samantha Toots's squeaks of remorse have been silenced by my eager mouth she becomes a different person. Everything I touch seems to send her into another fit of shuddering passion and when I greedily pull up her cotton sweater and turn my mitts loose on her bristols the reaction is, to put it mildly, electrifying. The whole row of seats threatens to work itself free of its moorings and, like a packet of fags left on the dashboard of a clapped out banger we are shaken onto the floor.

Recently, life has presented me with a few disappointments nooky-wise and I am keen that there should be no repetition of those thrust-quenching incidents which have left me with no more than a disappointed ruckle of the y-fronts to remember the what-might-have-been. For this reason I move with more than my usual speed and quickly wriggle free from the tacky embrace of my coffee-stained jeans. Beneath her long skirt Sam wears – absolutely nothing! The discovery fills me with a certain disquiet because it does not seem quite nice really. I may be old-fashioned but I do expect birds to wear a pair of knicks! I mean, it's more refined, isn't it?

Luckily Toots's tornado tactics help overcome my temporary distaste and I am soon rolling back her long skirt like you might fold down the neck of a sack. Her mouth is seldom an inch from mine and only leaves the sanctuary of my lips in order to plunder another part of my body. 'Oh yes,' she breathes, caressing Percy from P to Y, 'yes, yes, yes.'

I am in no mood to argue with her and with the smooth action of a twenty-five pounder shell sliding into the breech I close the distance between us to a number of hair breadths. Her mouth is open and her eyes are closed and I can see that one of her bottom teeth is a bit crooked. Funny that I should notice a thing like that at the moment like this.

Sam is one of those birds who is terrified of her own sensuality. Like an alcoholic circling a bottle of gin she knows that it only needs a taste for everything to go off the rails. Once she gives in – pow! Sex with Samantha is like trying to stay on a bucking bronco. After three minutes of being churned around on her hips I feel like an egg that has been whisked into a bowl of cake mix. Even when the lights go on I am not certain whether I am seeing it or feeling it. It is only when I recognise Justin's horrified mug staring down at me that I know I am seeing it.

'What the devil!?' says the short, fat geezer with him.

'O-o-o-o-o-o-o-h!!' The sounds from the back row suggest that something very beautiful has just come to an end, or, that an end has just come too – something beautiful. You pays your money and you takes your choice.

'Turn that bleeding light off!' snarls Sid as his face appears above the row of seats shortly followed by that of Sadie.

'Beryl!'

'Daddy!'

'Excuse me.' The last words are mine and accompanied by a hurried fumbling for my jeans. Reunions between father and daughter can often become very emotional affairs and I am not particularly big on sentiment myself. It would be better if I crept quietly –

'You swine!!!'

'Daddy, don't. Remember your heart.'

'Mr. Guttman, please!'

'Get out of my way! Let me get at him! You know what they do to tom cats!' I can see by the way Sidney moves that he knows all right.

'Mr. Guttman, Mr. Guttman, calm yourself,' shouts Justin. This gentleman is making a considerable investment in our next production. Right, Mr. Noggett?'

Sidney looks at the expression on Guttman's face and then begins to nod slowly.

'We need money from creatures like that?' sobs Guttman. 'Seducing my little girl. Look, she's been drugged. It's obvious.'

Sadie, or Beryl as I know her, is one of those birds you can never imagine ever having been a little girl and the thought of her being seduced does not fit easily into the mind. She does look drugged, though. It must be the booze.

'I assure you, Mr. Guttman. We were just having a bit of fun,' stammers Sid.

' "Fun!!" Seducing my little girl, "fun"? Where's this contract you were talking about? I'm going to tear it limb from limb.'

It occurs to me that nobody has mentioned a contract but Justin is swift to produce a folded sheet of paper which Guttman snatches from his hands.

'Mr. Guttman! I beg you to reconsider,' sobs Justin. 'What has happened here is highly reprehensible and I can appreciate your feelings of outrage at seeing your first-born in the process of despoliation but think of the longer view. Is it not right that this man should make good the wrong he has done? His signature on that contract can be a step towards financial reimbursement at least.'

'I feely dizzy. My throat is dry,' croaks Sadie.

'Drugged. He's drugged her. What did I tell you?' howls Guttman. 'Fetch the police! I will not rest until that twisted pervert is behind bars!'

'Relax! Relax!' shrieks Sid. 'I didn't drug anyone. I swear it. It was the girls' idea. Look, I'll sign it. Give me that piece of paper. Let's not get hysterical about this.'

He grabs the piece of paper and dashes off a signature so fast that his trousers fall down again.

Guttman extends his arms. 'What is the world coming to when I have to do business with rapists and perverts,

74

drug peddlers and sexual maniacs. Come, Rachel —'

'Beryl!' hisses Justin.

'— come Beryl. Let us go round to Great Portland Street and beg for atonement.' He snatches back the contract and sails out with Sadie hobbling into her skirt behind him. Justin pauses for a moment and shakes his head.

'A bad business,' he says solemnly. 'I'll see you later.' He is talking to Sam who is still lying on the floor with her hands over her head to shut out the noise.

'Look, Mr. Tymely —' Sidney hurries after Justin and Sam and I are left alone.

'Oh dear, says Sam. 'That was awful, wasn't it?'

'Awful,' I agree with her.

'Just when we were having such a lovely time, too.' She looks at me out of the corner of one of her eyes and smooths her skirt over her thigh.

'It was good, wasn't it?'

'Sometimes when something like that happens it's difficult to pick up the threads.' She pulls her sweater down so that her nipples jut out like bell pushes.

I suck in my breath. 'Yes.'

'What are we going to do now?'

'Where's the light switch in this place?' I ask her.

CHAPTER FIVE

'Of course, you were done, weren't you?'

'Look at that one. She's a bit of all right, isn't she?'

'I looked up Guttman in "Who's Who of the Screen" and he doesn't have a daughter.'

'Fantastic legs.'

'He couldn't even get her name right.'

'Blimey. I'd give her a part any day of the week.'

'You're not listening to me, are you, Sid? I'm telling you that you were conned. That scene in the projection booth was a put-up job to pressure you into signing the contract.'

'I put up as well, didn't I? I'm not grumbling. Don't worry, Timmo. We can't lose money on a film that has got chicks like that in it.'

It is a few days after our lunch with Justin and we are attending a casting session for Oliver Twist, this being the vehicle into which Sid has sunk a considerable amount of moola. Just how much, he did not realise until he got his copy of the contract. Certainly my memory of the conversation at the lunch table revolved around a figure approximately half of that which Sidney has now contracted to lash out.

At least Sidney is not the only backer of the movie and I am amazed at how many blokes there do seem to be in on the deal. About a dozen people have a slice of the action and most of them are attending the casting session.

'Sidney, I'd like you to meet Alma Mater. I think she'd make a wonderful Nancy.' Justin is introducing a tall, slim dark girl with straight shoulder-length hair and eyes that blaze like truck headlights. She is wearing a black leotard with a white apron – at least, that is the effect achieved.

'You've got enough Nancies around here already,

76

haven't you?' says Sidney, never slow to impress with his salty wit. 'Pleased to meet you, Nancy.'

'I hear you're one of the backers,' says Nancy. 'That's fantastic, that really is. I think people who put money into art are just unbelievable. I'm a dancer really, you know. I'm very lucky because I'm double-jointed and I can do things with my body that most other people can't begin to attempt. It really is a pleasure meeting you, Mr. Noggett, because I've heard so much about you. I hope you don't mind me going on like this but I feel I can talk to you. You have a sort of warm quality. You really come over, if you know what I mean?'

I am practically reaching for my vomit bag but Sidney, being the kind of stupid twit that he is, laps it all up like it is the flavour of the month. It is funny but Sidney can be quite effective when he is dishing out the chat. Give him some tongue-tied little bird and the words break over her in waves. When he is on the receiving end his mind seems to put on diving boots. I think it is because he reckons that all birds are stupid he never takes anything they say at anything other than face value. That is why my sister Rosie can put it across him so easily. Rosie used to be dumb but she has changed. Sidney has not. Funny how smart I used to think he was when I first met him.

'It's very nice of you to say so, Miss Mater,' says Sid awkwardly. 'I suppose one always tries to look for the best in people. Look – er, let's have a cup of coffee. I'd like to hear more about your dancing.'

He leads her away – or thinks he does – and I am left with Justin who has a satisfied expression on his mug.

'Going well, is it?' I ask allowing a trace of sarcasm to creep into my voice.

'Splendidly, Timothy. Quite splendidly. It may sound a trifle cynical but one does try to marry the action on the screen to real life. Those who invest money in our productions are often frustrated thespians and if we can transplant them into a relationship with some of the protagonists on the filmic level, then their reward is twofold. Do I make myself clear?'

'You mean if you put up some ackers you can get your end away with the cast?'

'Precisely. Or, at least, you stand a better chance of doing so.' Justin pats me on the back. 'Very good, Timothy. What a pity I've already cast the Artful Dodger.'

'Justin. There's one thing I don't understand. Why are we doing Oliver Twist. I mean, it's been flogged to death, hasn't it? There's the stage version and a couple of films –'

'Exactly Timothy! You put your finger on it. It's become a classic, you see. All great works are being revived the whole time. Look at the Bible. People are always making films and plays about it. It becomes a question of interpretation, searching for new meanings, revealing hidden truths. The creative process is a mirror capable of infinite representations of the same object.'

He is a lovely talker, Justin, there is no doubt about it. When I listen to him rabbiting on it makes me realise how ignorant I am. Also, how difficult it must be in the film industry if a person of his obvious genius has to make films like 'Up the Ladder, Jack' in order to scrape together a few bob. I suppose people like me should blame ourselves for not having superior tastes so that people like Justin can do things worthy of their talents.

'Another thing I don't understand, Justin,' I say apologetically, 'is why you seem to be casting so many birds. It's not a musical is it?'

'No, no. Good gracious me, no. No, I'm getting the women out of the way today, and casting the male characters tomorrow. Also,' – he looks round to see that no one is listening – 'I might as well be completely honest with you. Some of the backers, as you already surmised, do demand slightly more than their pound of flesh. Many of the girls here today have no chance of a part in the film – and know it.'

'Like Alma?' I venture.

'Precisely. Alma would have difficulty walking across the set without someone chalking out footsteps for her to follow. She has other talents.'

I get an inkling of what these talents might be the next day when Sidney limps into view with his earhole practically on his shoulder.

'That bird wasn't kidding when she said she was double jointed,' he croaks. 'Blimey, I didn't know whether I was coming or going. It quite put me off sometimes. I reckon she could have done me a serious injury.'

'You mean you took advantage of that poor star-struck child,' I scold him. 'Shame on you, Sid. How could you have done it?'

'Come off it, Timmo. She was crazy for it. It was the old Noggett magnetism driving her out of her mind into a hailstorm of torrid ecstasy.'

'You mean maelstrom, Sidney,' I tell him. 'Although I reckon it probably was more like a hailstorm. Little icy balls banging away –'

'Hey, wait a minute. Just because you're jealous, there's no need to be like that.'

Sidney is right. I am jealous. He is so blooming lucky that it makes me sick sometimes. I would not mind if he accepted it as good fortune and was grateful, but all this magnetism muck gets right up my bracket.

I am also feeling narky because Justin has told me that he will not be able to give me a credited part for fear that the union might cut up nasty. Blooming marvellous, isn't it? If it was not for me there probably would not be a film in the first place.

'Plenty of extra work, Timmo,' says Justin. 'Once everyone gets used to your face I can start exploiting your potential.'

'Don't get upset about it, ducky,' chips in Crispin. 'I started at the bottom.'

I have about half a dozen answers to that one but luckily the arrival of Mac, looking like the bearer of important news, prevents me from using them.

'He's here,' says Justin.

For the first time that I can remember, Justin looks less than totally at ease and I wonder who the new arrival can be. There is one dead simple way to find out.

'Who is?' I ask.

'Ken Loser,' breathes Justin.

'Never heard of him.'

'Never heard of him?! The most famous British director of the decade? Surely you've seen some of his television work. His series on the New Testament?'

'You mean when he had Jesus dressed up in a wet suit and flippers diving off the top of the Eiffel Tower? Yes, now you come to mention it, I do remember something about it. There were a lot of complaints, weren't there?'

'Only about the brothel scene. People are incredibly reactionary, you know. I thought it was very meaningful myself.'

'Very meaningful,' echoes Mac. 'It makes the point that Jesus is the Devil is Man more clearly than anything else I have ever found sexually stimulating.'

'He's going to direct the film, is he?' I ask.

'Yes. It's a fantastic coup,' breathes Justin. 'His presence alone ensures that we get our money back at the box office.'

We all look towards the door expectantly and through it come two enormous tawny hounds pulling a geezer in white chauffeur's uniform with jackboots and Nazi-style peaked cap. He is wearing dark glasses and has a long gold cigarette holder drooping from his lips.

'Is that him?' I gasp.

'No!' Justin's tone is almost contemptuous. 'That's Otto, his, his –'

'Personal assistant,' says Mac helpfully.

Stupid of me really but you do get these funny ideas about film people, don't you? Of course there is no reason why they should be any different to you or – 'Blimey!' My exclamation is sparked off by the next bloke to come through the door. He is wearing a shaggy sheepskin coat that drags along the floor behind him, and from the niff that sprints across the room you would reckon the sheep was still in there with him. He has matted shoulder length hair that makes Justin's coiffure look like that of a Sandhurst cadet, a wooden cross round his neck and open-toed

80

sandals revealing ten of the dirtiest little piggies that ever went 'wiggy, wiggy, wiggy, all the way home'. In his hand is a riding crop which he twirls impatiently.

'Ken!' says Justin expansively. 'Marvellous to see you.' He steps over one of the hounds which is pissing against his desk, and grabbing Loser's upper arm with one hand, pumps his mitt up and down with the other.

'I see this thing as totally nihilistic,' says Loser, shrugging him aside as if he did not exist. 'I want everything – the orgies, the rapes, the desecration, the infanticide, the underwater lesbianism, to bring every man, woman and child in the audience face to face with the fundamental question.'

There is a long pause in which Justin smiles and then nods briskly, as if having considered every aspect of what has just been said he is in total agreement with it.

'What fundamental question?' I ask.

'Exactly!!' Loser's whip crashes down on Justin's desk and the dogs bolt across the room pulling the geezer in the chauffeur's uniform over an armchair. 'That's the question, isn't it? The question is: What is the question? I am the only genius making films today who has got the guts to ask it!' He takes another swing at the desk, and throws his whip out of the window, before sinking into a chair and covering his face with his hands. 'I want a cast of nonentities. I want them unspoilt, untainted. I want to pillage their experiences, to plunge my arm down their throats and eviscerate them! There must be no preconceptions to come between them and the truth. No text, no words, no script, nothing! Nothing! Nothing!' He is practically sobbing as he snaps his fingers at his assistant. 'Cigarette!'

Otto nods and lights a cigarette which he inserts in the gold holder and passes to his master. Loser removes the fag and grinds it out on the back of his hand. 'Only my third today,' he says triumphantly, 'I'm cutting down.'

Blimey, but there are some funny people about aren't there? Justin gets rid of me saying that he has some business matters to discuss with Loser and as I go through the door I see the great man tucking into a bacon sandwich he has produced from somewhere inside his sheepskin. I know the British Film Industry is going through a bad time but this is ridiculous!

The next exciting star of stage, screen and labour exchange that I meet is Glint Thrust. He is undoubtedly one of the best looking blokes that I have ever seen and also, I reckon, one of the best looking blokes that he has ever seen. His nostrils are permanently flared and his piercing eyes filled to the brim with a kind of distant loathing as if he has just trodden in something too unspeakable to think about in the middle of the duchess's sitting room. He is very big on suède and moves around stiffly as if his underpants are made of it. All the birds on the set think the M.G.M. lion roars through his backside and he is not slow to capitalise on the fact. He has his own special caravan and is disposed to retire to it between takes, with a different dolly on each occasion. It is fantastic the number of birds he goes through and they say that he has 'comfort breaks' as he calls them, written into his contract.

'I've got to keep in shape,' he keeps mumbling, flinging his arm about. 'Booze and broads, that's what does it. They don't call me Glint Thrust because of the way I stick stamps on envelopes.'

As he himself says, booze is another of Glint Thrust's consuming interests and he gets through so much that you feel he must have parked his corpuscles in a blood bank to make room for it. How he remembers his lines is beyond me, but luckily, under Ken Loser's direction he does not need many of them. At first I am surprised to see Glint Thrust in the film after what Loser has said in Justin's office but after watching a few takes I can understand why Loser maintains that he is the biggest nonentity in the business. He is always scratching himself or the nearest chick and keeps nodding with his eyes closed and mumbling 'yep, yep yep,' every time Loser says anything to him.

The other key 'property' as Justin persists in calling her,

is Dawn Lovelost, who I remember seeing on tele about the time you had it facing the street so all the neighbours knew you had one. Her face is a water-colour of a once beautiful woman painted in something a lot stronger than water. Like Glint she fancies a drop of the hard stuff and, it is rumoured, is also quite fond of a drop of the hard. Certainly four marriages suggest that she has more than a passing acquaintance with the old spam ram.

I am surprised to find that Sandra does not have a part in the movie but Justin explains that big tits are anti-culture and down market.

'Show me one classical actress with big tits,' he says. 'Dame Sybil Thorndike, Edith Evans, Dulcie Gray; not a spare ounce of flesh on any of them.'

Sid is still chuffed to bollocks because he is now an impresario or 'Empress aerial' as he prefers to call it.

'What I like about it, Timmo,' he explains, 'is that it's culture, isn't it? I mean, I wasn't too keen on all that nudie-pics nonsense when you started telling me about it, but this is different. I mean, I don't mind watching films like that, but I don't want to get mixed up in making them, do I?'

'How's your neck, Sidney?'

'Better, Timmo. But, like I was saying. One of the greatest classics in the English language. Can't be bad, can it? My name up there. Patron of the arts. It might be the first step toward a knighthood or a life peerage. Lord Noggett of Clapham. How does that grab you?'

That's what I like about Sidney. For a medium-sized, pot-bellied geezer bearing a faint resemblance to Paul Newman in a bad light, he does think big.

'Very nice,' I tell him. 'Rosie is going to like that, isn't she?'

For a second Sid's face clouds over and I see him looking warily at Glint Thrust who is padding off towards his caravan with an evil flicker in his eye and an eager extra in his grasp.

'Yeah. We'll have to watch her with old Lightning Tonk, won't we? You know how she can be sometimes.'

I do indeed. As already mentioned, she has broadened her horizons a lot since she first snagged her tights in the back of Sid's mini-van and her attitude to men of the opposite sex has veered between the friendly and the 'come and get it!' Not, of course, that Sidney has the word 'restraint' tattooed across his scrotum but, as we all know, it is different for men.

Sidney's fears are well founded as I see when the Lady Rosie visits the set. She takes one look at Glint and freezes like a gundog scenting a victim. He rolls his eyeballs over her and you could .draw dotted lines between their two sets of peepers. If they were both dogs I would push off and start filling a bucket of water. Luckily Glint has to react in front of the cameras so an immediate confrontation is avoided.

'Right, Glint. Listen,' says Loser, whose sheepskin coat does not smell any better under the arc lights, 'let me feel this one with you.' Glint is still looking at Rosie and he nods as if he likes the idea. 'Let's re-establish your motivation. You are a committed socialist who has been crushed into poverty and insignificance by the jackboot of reactionary capitalism. You steal, murder and rape because this is your way of crying for help, of focusing public attention on your predicament and the wrongs that a grossly lop-sided, misguided society has perpetrated upon you.'

'Dig,' says Glint, nodding. 'I bash her about a bit and then ram it up her.'

'And we dissolve into the lyrical scene with you as a little boy playing with your dog on the hills above the Welsh mining village. Exactly. Are you ready, Dawn?'

Dawn Lovelost is fiddling with something in the area of her ample bristols.

'This isn't real blood, is it?' she says distastefully.

'Of course it's real blood,' snaps Loser. 'Not real human blood –' a slight note of disappointment creeps into his voice, 'but real sheep's blood. Try and turn towards the camera so that we can come right in on it spurting from your chest. O.K., Mac?'

'O.K., K.L.'

Loser turns back to Dawn. 'And get your mouth really wide open when you scream. I want the camera to disappear down your throat.'

'Ooh! Sounds horrible!' says Rosie. Unfortunately, she says it out loud.

'Of course it's horrible, you stupid bitch!' howls Loser. 'Life is horrible. What do you think I'm trying to say? What good is art if it doesn't make you feel. To vomit is to feel. After one of my movies I want people to come out into the street puking! Physically and mentally different. Their minds expanded, reorientated. Any artistic endeavour that does not challenge basic conceptions about life is fart, not art!'

Many women might be distressed into silence by such an attack, but not our Rosie. Fortunately she has no idea what Loser is on about, but she does understand words like 'fart' and 'bitch'.

'Don't you talk to me like that,' she snorts. 'Do you know who I am?'

'I know what you are,' yells Loser. 'You're a soft-brained, overdressed, underwitted pawn of creeping bourgeois mediocrity who has the snivelling impertinence to interrupt a genius in the execution of his duty to posterity. Otto! Set the dogs on her!'

Quick on the uptake readers will sense that things are on the verge of getting out of hand and it is as well that Justin calls a ten-minute break and walks Loser round the stage a couple of times to cool down.

I am about to perform a similar service for Rosie when Glint Thrust appears with the unwanted inevitability of a noisy fart at the vicar's tea party.

'I felt I just had to come and say how awful I felt about you being talked to like that,' he gushes. 'That man may be a genius but he can be a real pig most of the time.'

'He had no call to go on like that,' sniffs Rosie. 'Look, he's made me cry. My make-up will be all over the place.'

'Fix yourself up in my dressing room,' husks Glint, extending a hand. 'We might even have a little drink to soothe your nerves.'

It is not half-past ten yet and I do not think it is in anyone's interest to get Glint and Rosie curled up alongside a bottle of booze at this hour in the morning.

'Mind your own business,' she snaps when I make a few respectful observations on the subject. 'I didn't hear you standing up for me when that terrible man insulted me. Wait 'til Sidney hears about this.'

That thought is occurring to me, though in a slightly different context. Few ladies merge from Glint's caravan without their knickers making a quick trip down to ankle level and Rosie is not one of the least sociable birds in the world when you get a couple of vodkas and orange inside her. Should things get out of hand and Sidney stumble across a big feature starring his lady wife, then my career in pictures could be right up the spout. I must take steps to ensure that no opportunity for sexual congress arises.

All the curtains in Glint's caravan are drawn so I wait a couple of minutes and then knock on the door. Glint has his jacket off and is not pleased to see me.

'Are we rolling again?' he asks.

'No, Mr. Thrust, but I wondered if I could have your autograph for my kid sister.'

'Listen, boy. You know the rules. Don't interrupt me when I'm recovering. I give a lot out there, you know.' I peer over his shoulder to see if Rosie has started giving anything yet. Luckily she still appears to be fully clothed. She sticks her tongue out at me.

'I'm sorry, Mr. Thrust. It's just that she's such a big fan and I know that –'

'O.K., O.K.! Give me the book.'

It suddenly occurs to me that I don't have a book.

'If you write it backwards onto my hand I'll press it on a piece of blotting paper,' I bleat helplessly.

'Get out!'

The door slams in my face and I am left to plan my next move. Five minutes later I have found a hammer and go round the caravan tapping the wheels and anything else that looks as if it joins on to something.

'Now what?!' Thrust is standing at the top of the steps and looking less inviting than an invitation to your mother-in-law's for Christmas.

'Just checking that everything is in shape for the road,' I say cheerfully, noticing that Glint's shirt is now unbuttoned to the waist and his face flushed.

'It never goes on the road,' snarls Thrust. 'But you will in a minute unless you make yourself scarcer than horseshit on the M.1.' He slams the door shut and the whole caravan shudders.

Oh dear! Unless Loser comes back sharpish things could get very sticky. Fortunately, as always seems to happen at such moments, I have an idea. Loser's hounds are lashed to a prop at the end of the studio and showing every sign of wanting to go for walkies. Otto is having a very earnest chat with Crispin:

'Just love the feel of it against my skin,' he is saying as I approach. 'If I had my way I'd never wear anything else.'

'Can I take the dogs for a walk?' I ask.

'Careful they don't take you for a walk, dear,' says Otto. 'Really. My arms are just a mass of muscles from being dragged about by those brutes.'

'Go on!' says Crispin, 'you're not the muscly type. You must weigh under a hundred and fifty pounds.'

'Spot on! You are clever.'

'I used to be a masseur once. Worked in a Turkish bath. I bet if I ran my hands over you I would be able to tell within a couple of pounds how much you weighed.'

'What, with my clothes on?'

'You'd have to give me a little latitude with your clothes on.'

'Ooh, cheeky!'

I leave them to it and untie the dogs. By the cringe, but they are powerful brutes. I can see what Otto was on about. I can practically tuck my hands in the top of my socks by the time the dogs have pulled me through the door. They point a hind leg skywards and make a brave attempt to drill a hole in the side of the building and I drag them back on the set again. Still no sign of Ken Loser or Sidney. God knows what is happening in that caravan. I am certain I can hear panting as I approach it, but maybe it is the dogs. There are a couple of chocks under the wheels and I tap these aside before tying the frisky pooches to the coupling mechanism of the caravan. Coupling mechanism. Oh, my gawd! I steal down the side of the caravan and raise my head to peep through a chink in the tightly drawn curtains. No! I am almost too late. Thrust and Rosie are assaulting each other's mouths as if trying to spread their lips over a wider area of face. At least they are still upright but – oh no! Even as I look Rosie is being pushed back on to a folding table and Thrust's hands are opening up new territory. I tear my eyes away from this disgusting sight and hiss at the dogs to perform a swift giddy-up. But, not a sausage. Having cocked Charlie at the corrugated iron they are now content to slump down and let their ridiculous tongues loll out of their mouths like tired tonks. There is a vague tremor coming from the caravan but this is more likely to be the work of Thrust and Rosie than anything sparked off by the pooches. The thought makes me move even faster and I hare out of the studio in search of something capable of making the dogs get their paws out. If only – ah! There padding majestically across the asphalt in front of me is a large, long-haired moggy.

'Oo's a luvly pussy, den?' I yodel. 'Come to nunky Timmy for strokums. 'Oo's a booful boy?'

Sheer, naked nausea, but the old cat arches its back and wanders over all ready for the big touch up. Just shows how careful you should be about talking to strangers. I sweep it into my arms and am legging it back to the set before you can say 'cheap fur coats'. My new friend does not like this very much but I keep it bundled up underneath my jacket and few of the scratches I receive are more than a quarter of an inch deep.

The caravan is definitely rocking when I return and I fear the worst. Fortunately the camera crew are all reading their Beanos or playing cards so I am not under anyone's eagle eye. Pausing only to take a quick shufti round the set, I remove my long-haired help-mate and drop her a few yards in front of the dogs. Boy! If I was expecting something to happen I am not disappointed. The hair on the moggy's back goes straight up in the air and her back arches like an inverted U. One of the pooches nearly breaks its neck hurling itself against its lead and they both set up a furious barking. The cat moves like shit off a shovel and the dogs practically make grooves in the concrete scrabbling to get after it. For a second the caravan trembles and then lurches forward as a shout of surprise and laughter goes up from the crew.

'Wagons Roll!' There are yells and a terrified scream that seems to come from inside the caravan. This coincides with that object entering the Cock Tavern or rather attempting to enter it. The flimsy set collapses under the impact, and plywood and scaffolding rain down upon those playing gin rummy beneath. The caravan is now building up a healthy momentum of its own and has almost overtaken the dogs when it crunches into the side wall of the studio. The dogs leap and bay but there is no budging it.

'My gawd! Those bloody dogs!'

'It was a bleeding cat what set them off.'

'Blooming heck!' The last words come from Sidney who appears striding past me towards the lop-sided caravan.

'Sidney,' I pipe. 'Oh, Sidney.'

Sidney turns on me. 'Yes?'

Desperately, I searched for something to say. 'Er, um. Do you want me to go first?'

'Don't be soft.' Sidney shakes his head and throws open the door of the caravan. I suck in my breath. What hideous scene of noo (interrupted nooky) is going to bombard my mince pies? Will Sidney's incensed eyes feed upon the form of his loved one still stretched out on the serving hatch. Is service being maintained, even in these trying conditions?

As anticipated, Glint is in the process of zipping up his

action man kit while trying to keep his feet amongst the shambles.

'Are you O.K., Glint?'

'I'll tell you when my lawyer gets here,' snaps our lovable leading man. 'What the hell's been going on? Did this simpering idiot have anything to do with it?'

He means me, but I am not listening. Where the hell has Rosie got to? While Sidney makes with the mumbles my eyes are combing the room for a sight of her lovely form. There is no space for her to hide and she can't have – wait a moment! Poking out from a closed cupboard door is a scrap of material I recognise. Rosie's dress. And it is not a cupboard door. It is the home of a foldaway bed. Poor Rosie! What a way to go. A big girl like her could suffocate in there. I must get Sidney out double-quick. I turn to him and see to my horror that he has also registered the bit of Rosie's dress. I can practically hear the cogs in his mind knitting together as he tries to place it.

'Better get outside, Mr. Thrust,' I say thoughtfully. 'You must be pretty shaken up.'

'Yeah,' says Mr. Loathsome. 'I'll just fix myself a shot of tranquilliser and I'll be right out. You fellows needn't hang around.' He advances purposefully to the door closes it behind us.

'Could have been very nasty, that,' says Sid seriously. 'We were dead lucky there, really.'

'Too true, Sidney,' I agree with him. 'Too true.'

CHAPTER SIX

'Have you noticed how pale Rosie is looking these days?' says Sidney the morning after the caravan incident.

'She doesn't get out enough,' I tell him. 'Spends too much time cooped up indoors.'

'You're right,' says Sid. 'I'll have a word with her about it. There's no reason why she shouldn't take Jason and Nicholas to the Cromby for a bit.

Nicholas is the infant sprog Noggett so named virtually over my dead body. I mean! Nicholas Noggett! It sounds like a novel by Monica Dickens, doesn't it? Not that there is much you can put with Noggett that does not sound ridiculous or dead common. Sid's children would be better off just having initials.

'You do that, Sidney,' I say. 'And now, if you will excuse me, I have to go and get kitted out for my part.'

Sidney winces because he is dead jealous that I am appearing in the picture. He would be happy for me to be clapper boy if he thought I was going to catch my dick in the board. He keeps ranting on about lashing out money as if the whole of his investment in the movie was going into my pocket.

The scene I am appearing in takes place in the recently restored Cock Tavern and features Bill Sikes and Nancy becoming acquainted over a few beers. I am only just getting used to the fact that none of the scenes are being shot in sequence and, in fact, we seem to be making the film backwards.

Besides Glint Thrust and Dawn Lovelost, who loathe each other, there are a large number of extras including some very handsome chicks none the worse for wearing off the shoulder costumes which are practically off everything. We are supposed to represent the tavern regulars and Ken Loser picks up a megaphone and ascends a stepladder to tell us what to do.

'You are suppressed, reviled, downtrodden, miserable and helpless,' he tells us. 'Above all you are hungry. A hunger of the spirit as well as of the body. Your only food is each other's mouths to be seized, devoured, fed upon in a manner the enlightened watcher can only regard as cannibalistic – evidence of how working-class solidarity is starved to death by inhuman capitalism. Yes, what is it?' He breaks off to address one of the studio security men who has appeared at the foot of his ladder.

'Excuse me, Mr. Loser, sir, but your Rolls is blocking the entrance to the staff canteen.'

'Don't interrupt me while I'm creating, you numb-skull!' snarls Loser, 'see my chauffeur. My God! Did Eisenstein have to put up with this?' Nobody seems to know the answer to that one so he continues with his instruction. 'So remember, use your bodies like weapons. When you embrace you are preying on each other. Your lips are wine, your bodies bread. Devour! Devour! Devour!'

I must say Loser knows how to get results. The clapper boy has not finished doing his stuff before a big, dark bird pulls me on to her mouth like I am an oxygen mask, and tries to suck all my teeth out. For a moment I am a bit taken aback but a glance round the set tells me that nobody else is bothering to exchange visiting cards so I get stuck in with a will – or willy as it is more commonly known. Really! Some of the things that are going on about me I would not credit if they were happening at a Young Conservatives' wine and cheese party, let alone in front of a dirty great movie camera. People seem to have no shame these days. I have not seen so much groping since grandma's dentures rolled under the table at Aunty Helen's silver wedding knees-up and dad went after them with Mrs. Blackburn. The miserable old git is a completely different proposition with a few ales inside him as Mrs. B. found out to her cost.

'Combine! Conjoin,' bellows Loser through his mega-puhone. 'You're hungry, savage beasts rebelling against a million years of serfdom!'

'Oh baby, baby!' groans the bird I am grappling with, 'do it to me! Do it to me!' I must say that with all the writhing bodies around me and Loser doing an Ike Turner through his megaphone, the prospect does seem one not to be sniffed at.

'To think we get paid for this,' I pant as I feel my friend's rearside shock absorbers bouncing against my tightening fingers.

'It's extra for physical contact,' groans the chick. 'The union demands it.'

The union is not the only one, I think to myself as strong female fingers plunder Percy's private pad. I turn my head and the couple next to me are actually having it away on the trestle table.

'Have you ever worked for Ken before?' breathes my friend; 'he's fantastic – he gets things out of you that you never knew you had.'

My dark-haired chum is obviously a lady after Loser's own heart, although I knew I had what she is getting out.

'O.K., cut!' howls Loser. I sit up obediently but around me the set is still a writhe riot.

'CUT!!' Still not a sausage. The couple on the table seem to have gone into orbit.

'Oh baby, let's use it while we've got it,' pants my eager little friend. 'We're just two grains of sand on the beach of time. Tomorrow we'll be infinity.' This is a subject I would like to discuss further but Loser roars down his step ladder and starts breaking up the action with his riding crop.

'Cut! Cut! Cut!' he hollers. 'There's plenty of time for that in the deathbed scene.'

'Too bad,' says my chum giving my old man an affectionate squeeze. 'Maybe we'll meet in the next orgy.'

'I'll keep my fly open for you,' I say wittily.

'That was a bit saucy, wasn't it?' says Sid when I speak to him a few minutes later.

'It didn't worry you at all?'

'What do you mean?'

'Well, you don't think all that groping and stuff is a bit – er, well?'

'Not if it's art, Timmo. I have no complaints at all. Mr. Tymely explained all about Mr. Loser and how he is trying to liberate the hidden meaning of the subtext and how he is seeking to shock people out of their complacency. I think it's very good. He's socially committed, you see. As long as the sex and violence is used for a didactic purpose it must be all right, mustn't it?'

It is obvious that Sidney has been nobbled. Words like 'subtext' and 'didactic' fall from his gob more rarely than pig's trotters from a horse chestnut tree.

'It can't be bad for raking in a few shekels at the box office either, can it?'

Sidney shakes his head as if wounded. 'You look too closely for the profit motive sometimes, Timmo,' he says sadly. 'There are other things you know.'

I feel like being very unkind and asking him for a list of three that does not include moola but am prevented by being called back to the set. This time I am forming part of the background to a scene featuring Bill Sikes and Nancy, or Glint Thrust and Dawn Lovelost as their agents call them – which is probably very rarely.

As already mentioned, Glint and Dawn find it marvellously easy to resist each other and their only interest is booze. When not trying to ram his nasty up anything in a skirt that does not talk with a Scots accent and wear a sporran, Glint is frequently to be observed holding a bottle of the hard stuff at an angle of forty-five degrees above his parched lips. Dawn is more discreet in her booze intake and takes most of her snifters in her dressing room where all her scent bottles are rumoured to be full of brandy.

Whatever the source of intake there is no doubt that both Glint and Dawn have had a very adequate ration of liquor before coming on to the set and a whiff of their breath would be enough to kill a St. Bernard's sense of smell stone dead for three weeks. In such a condition it might be persuaded to rescue Ken Loser, whose sheepskin is currently ponging something rotten.

'Right, Lovelost,' says the ageing boy genius, favouring Dawn's shoulder with his arm. 'I want you to give everything you've got.'

'Is that the best she can do?' sneers Glint.

'Shut your face you piggish lout,' snaps Dawn. 'Why don't you concentrate on remembering your lines or, better still, write them on the back of a whisky bottle so you'll always have them with you.'

'Darlings, keep this tension. This is wonderful,' hisses Loser. 'Now Dawn, remember. First the knife through his hand pinning it to the table, then the mulled wine in his face. Glint, grab her by the hair and drag her across the table. You revile her then kiss her. Hold it while we pan from the kiss to the blood spurting from your hand. Have you got that, Mac?'

'Got it.'

'Extras crowd round as the knife goes in. Emote, erupt.'

'Interrelate?' says a voice hopefully.

'If you want to, but the camera will be on the protagonists. Right, ready? Roll 'em.'

'Blimey,' murmurs the extra sitting next to me. 'This coffee tastes like cold piss.'

'So today it's cold.'

'Yeah. But I've never known it taste like this.'

'Where did you get it from?'

'From the urn. Blimey. Do you know what I think? They've put the stuff that's supposed to be mulled wine in the urn and the coffee –'

'Oo-o-o-o-oow!' My friend is right. Glint collects a face full of hot coffee and his scream shakes the dust off the roof girders. 'You bitch!!' Dawn cops a meaty left-hander.

'You sod!!' Dawn's fingers rake Glint's cheek.

'Filthy whore!' Glint has both hands round her throat and is shaking hard.

'You're impotent! Impotent! Impotent!'

'How dare you,' shrieks Glint. 'They call me "stud"!'

'It should be "collar-stud" from all accounts,' croaks Dawn.

'Cut!' shouts Loser. 'That was beautiful, beautiful! What a performance! I haven't seen such acting since we set fire to Joan of Arc for real. O.K., Glint, you can put her down now. I said "put her down." Glint! Glint!'

Eventually three of us manage to pull Thrust off her and he is carried away to his caravan demanding a bottle of scotch wrapped up in a warm starlet.

Dawn is less easily comforted and moans fitfully for almost ten minutes before we can get her onto her feet. During that time she has 'sipped' her way through three tumblers of neat brandy.

'What fantastic commitment,' burbles Loser. 'I feel like a lightning conductor.'

It is occurring to me that this geezer is definitely round the twist and I wonder how long it is going to be before Sidney tumbles to the same conclusion. Several thousand pounds later as usual, I expect.

We lead Miss Lovelost back to her dressing room and I am fortunate enough to get my first supporting role on the left hand side of her body. This is in good shape and an ideal match for the right hand side of her soft and curvy frame. The upholstery may be on the move, but there is no doubt about the class of the article underneath.

'Wait a minute,' she wheezes as I attempt to follow my helpmate from her presence. 'Can you give me a glass of water before you go?'

Naturally, such a request is well within my power and I watch with interest as she applies a trace of brandy flavouring to 'take the taste away' as she puts it. When I say trace I mean about enough to drown a guinea pig in. 'Thank you, darling,' she breathes – and what a breath. 'I haven't seen you before, have I?' This is always a difficult question to answer but I nod agreeably and grant my eyes the freedom of her battered bodice.

'Oh dear, I'm popping out all over the place,' says Dawn. 'Still, I'm certain you've seen worse.'

'Oh, much worse,' I assure her. 'In fact I'd say you had a lovely figure.'

'You should have seen me when I was first discovered. I

was known as "The Made to Measure" girl. Betty Grable's legs, Jane Russell's bosom –' 'Trigger's thirst,' I think to myself. 'Men beat a path to my door. They had to pile the flowers outside my dressing room for fear they'd use up all the oxygen.'

'Not a word of that surprises me,' I say. 'I only wish I had a handful of blooms to thrust before you at this moment.'

I always find it easy to chatter to birds when they are pissed because in that condition I reckon they are not suddenly going to turn round and say 'what are you on about, you stupid berk?' With a chick who is totally compos mentis, my natural inferiority complex and fear of rebuff makes me more wary and tongue-tied. Fascinating, isn't it? O.K., so you don't go in for deep psychological insights. See if I care.

'You're sweet,' murmurs Dawn touching me lightly with her hand. 'It's comforting to know that everybody on this awful movie isn't a complete savage. Help yourself to a drink, darling.'

I ferret around for a glass and fix myself a small brandy. Experience of this kind of situation suggests to me that Miss Lovelost may be on the point of seeking comfort for the inner woman.

'Cheers!'

'Cheers!'

'You don't find my disarray too distracting?'

'I do, but in the nicest possible way.'

'You are a sweet boy. Very, very sweet.' With these encouraging words she slides an arm round my neck and draws me down onto her generous mouth. When I say generous, I mean, like it is trying to give me a second tongue. I don't know whether it is the power of her kissing or the smell of brandy on her lips but I feel as if I am passing out in a burning refinery.

'That was nice, wasn't it?' she murmurs, allowing me to escape for air. 'Why don't you turn the key in the lock? I don't want to be disturbed while we're talking.'

I have not been conscious of a lot of rabbit in the last

few moments but I do not argue the point. This lady may well have much to teach a struggling young actor. I have always been prepared to bend over backwards in order to enjoy the fruits of other people's experience. I dart across the room to perform the small service required of me and, from the door, treat her to a look of brooding intensity borrowed from an old Laurence Olivier film I saw on tele. She extends a graceful arm and it is obvious that we are going to make beautiful music together.

'Don't move,' I murmur. 'I always want to remember you like that.'

'Come to me, you foolish boy,' she burbles. 'Don't you realise this is madness?'

'If this is madness then I envy every lunatic in the world.' I collide with her cakehole and we enjoy the kind of kiss that would have been cut by fifteen seconds when Lassie was a puppy and still have had the film picketed by the Clapham Women's Institute. Suddenly she breaks away and turns her head dramatically to one side.

'But it can't work. We're being fools. Blind, stupid fools.'

'Because you're a rich, beautiful, talented star with fantastic knockers and I'm only a struggling extra? That's no reason why we can't snatch our moment of happiness. Oh, Dawn, Dawn. This was meant to be. It was written in the sky.' If only one had music this could be really beautiful but unfortunately the only accompaniment is supplied by one of the grips turning up his transistor to get the racing results.

'We can't!'

'We can!'

'We shouldn't!'

'We must!'

'Oh, Rupert!'

'Dawn!'

I don't know where she gets the Rupert from and I don't care very much either. Probably one of the old movies she starred in. With practised ease she sinks back along the sofa and raises one knee so that the outline of her thigh swells temptingly. As my mouth adjusts to her new position, I drop my hand to her ankle and move it lightly up her extended leg under cover of her long skirt. Her skin is as soft as the inside of a tenderised marshmallow and I feel Percy lurching forward eagerly as my fingers send back the glad tidings. Fantastic thing, the human body, isn't it? Just by looking at something you can make instant bone. Dawn's hand slides round behind my neck and her fingers entwine themselves deep in my hair as she moulds my mouth against hers. I am now getting so used to the brandy fumes that I am hardly aware of them. Catching an eyeful of tempting tit I start to withdraw my mitt in order to get to grips with it but Dawn pins my pandy between her thighs and joggles them up and down in a gesture rather more inviting than an 'at home' card from your friendly local abattoir. Always try to keep the customer satisfied, is one of the golden rules I learned at my father's knee – in fact it was somebody else's knee I learned it at, but that is another story – as the builder said when his client asked him where the bedrooms were.

I move my trusty left hand forward, wondering idly how many battalions of fingers have passed this way before, and silently congratulate Charlie Dickens on having written his immortal classic before tights were invented. How delightful not to have to risk breaking your wrists when indulging in a spot of digit dunking. Encouraging moans suggest that Dawn likes what is happening at lap level, as does the eager pressure of her fingers against the front door of my brushed-denim flare-bottoms. Oh dear! Times without count I have bemoaned the lack of self-jettisoning clobber which could be instantly shed at moments like this, but the manufacturers refuse to do anything about it. There is nothing more passion pricking than trying to preserve physical contact whilst struggling out of skin-tight threads.

In the present situation I join Dawn on her couch and we entwine our arms and make a brave attempt to un-lumber each other. Dawn's dress is laced in at the back like a corset and I make no more impression on it than I would on a roll of chicken wire. Dawn has an easier task and Percy bounces out to make new friends before you can say Roger Carpenter. So far, so average but, capable performer that she is, Dawn cannot get my jeans below thigh level and I eventually have to disengage myself and finish the job.

'That's enough,' says Dawn. Sensitive readers need not alarm themselves as I did for a moment. What she means is that enough articles of clothing have been removed for sexual congress to be joined. This is not strictly true in her case but after a rhythmic twist of the wrist and a little help from her arched back I am able to introduce her panties to my discarded y-fronts. Now all that stands between us and our deserved ration of ecstasy is whoever it is tapping on the door of the dressing room.

'Are you feeling all right?' says Justin's voice. 'Yes' would be my answer to that one as Dawn's petal pandies pop Percy into her pork pantry.

'I'm feeling better.'

'Is there anything you need?'

'I've got all I want at the moment, thank you, darling.' Dawn winks at me and pulls me closer, gritting her teeth.

'I'll have you called in ten minutes.'

'Make it twenty, darling. I need every second I can get.'

'O.K., darling,' calls Justin. 'Don't let it get on top of you.'

Half an hour later I am on the set feeling exhausted but elated. Under the spotlights Dawn is doing her thing and I can bathe in the satisfaction of thinking that a few minutes before I was doing it too. There can't be many extras who have had a star role – or roll – in their first picture.

'Did you have a nice time?' I am being whispered at by a thin, long-haired youth with a complexion so bad that the pimples are queuing up for vacant pores.

'What do you mean?' I hiss.

'You were having it off with Fanny Freelove, weren't you?'

The age of romance has obviously snuffed it. 'What do you mean?'

'Come off it. I saw you go in there. And I saw you when you came out. She doesn't only make the movie, that one. She makes everybody on the set as well. She uses blokes like corn plasters.'

'Who told you that?' I snarl, feeling not a little aggrieved to think that my experience has been by no means novel.

'Nobody told me. I found out the hard way.' The odious little jerk nudges me in the ribs. 'Do you get it? "Hard" way.'

I am still dead narked that evening when I return to Scraggs lane with Sidney. We are putting up there, or as Sidney has it: putting up with it there. Dad obviously returns the feeling.

'How's bleeding Lilian Gish today, then?' he says, flicking my hair contemptuously. 'How's the audience supposed to know whether you're a girl or a feller?'

'He keeps waving his dick at the camera,' says Sid. 'Come off it, dad. Why don't you leave him alone?'

'You mind your own bleeding business, sponger,' snarls dad. 'It's marvellous, isn't it? You can afford to make bleeding films but you can't lay out a few bob on a hotel room. Oh, no. It's round to Rosie's mum and dad with a box of Maltesers – not even bleeding After Eights.'

'I thought you encouraged show-biz personalities around here. What about little Jason?'

'That's different. He's flesh and blood, isn't he?'

'What do you think I am, mashed potatoes?'

'You know what I mean. He's one of the family. He's Rosie's kid.'

'Yeah, but I'm his dad. Doesn't that count for anything?'

'Not with me it doesn't. You haven't got any of my blood inside you.'

'What a disgusting thought. I reckon if you ever became a blood donor they'd be pushed to find anyone to give your stuff to.'

'Don't worry mate. I wouldn't give you none. Not if you were going baggy at the knees.'

'Charming!' says mum. 'That's not a very nice thing to say is it? I don't like all this talk about blood when I'm trying to eat.'

' "Trying" is the operative word,' says Sid. 'This bit of liver, I mean – it is liver, I suppose?'

''Course it is,' snorts dad. 'What did you think it was, shoe leather?'

'Now you come to mention it,' says Sid, putting down his fork and snapping his fingers, 'that's exactly what I was thinking. Either that or one of those stick-on rubber soles.'

'Don't you like it well done, dear?' says Mum.

'Not so you could light the fire with it. I mean, you know that Bisto we went to the other day, Timmo?'

'Bistro.'

'Yeah, like I said. Well, those Italians knew how to cook kidneys and liver and stuff like that, didn't they? All the natural juices were still there.'

'Don't be disgusting!' snarls dad. 'And don't talk to me about Eyeties. I had enough of them during the war.'

'Yeah, I remember. You were the only prisoner of war they ever took, weren't you?'

'I thought you spent all your time fire-watching,' I chip in.

'Sitting in front of the fire in an armchair. That's all the fire watching he ever did.'

'Don't you talk to me about the war, sonny,' dad's finger starts waving under Sidney's nose. 'I'm not going to bandy words with you on that subject.'

'Bandy legs, that's more your mark.'

'Shut up! I've had enough of being insulted in my own home. If you don't like it here, push off! I've said that to you a hundred times.'

'Would you like some more liver, dear?' says mum. Sidney buries his face in his hands and shakes it slowly from side to side.

'I'll have it, mum,' I say quickly. Being raised on mum's cooking has given me the constitution of a rock lizard.

'All this film business,' grumbles dad. 'When are we going to see something, then? I've never heard of any of these people. Ken Loser. Who's he when he's at home?'

'Just about the biggest talent in pictures today, that's all,' snorts Sid. 'Even you must have seen some of the stuff he's done on the tele.'

'All that blasphemous muck, was it? All that sex and violence. That's not how I remember "Little Women".'

'Yeah, but you watched to the bitten end, didn't you? I didn't see your hand sneaking out for the knob. Not that one anyway.'

'It's true, dad, I say hurriedly. 'He's – er, a very talented bloke.'

'I'll believe it when I see it,' grunts dad.

'I'd like to show you him in action,' says Sid, 'but he's very strict about visitors on the set. He had a bit of a barney with Rosie.'

'We heard about that,' says mum. 'He said some terrible things.'

'It's the same with all these highly-strung artistic people,' says Sid. 'They're very edgy. Little things upset them.'

'It is a pity,' says mum. 'I've always wanted to see the inside of a film studio. All those cameras and lights and things.

'Well,' says Sid. 'There's no reason why you shouldn't see round the studio when they're not shooting. You can do that any time. Like now, if you like.'

'Ooh! Do you hear that, father? That does sound exciting,' squeaks mum. 'Better than the tele, eh? I'll just serve up the sweet then we can be off. What would you like, Sidney? Bread and butter pudding or semolina?'

'I think if we're going back to the studio I'd better fill the car up,' says Sid rising hurriedly. 'I'll pick you all up in ten minutes.'

Sidney has made a wise decision, as anybody who has tackled mum's semolina would be the first to admit. The only good thing about it is the dollop of jam, and I always save that 'til last as a reward for not throwing up.

Despite the fact that we tell her nobody is going to be there, mum still spends twenty minutes tarting herself up and is in a rare state of excitement as she settles down in the back of Sidney's Rover 2000. Dad is obviously choked at having to give Sid best at anything and starts complaining about the positioning of the ashtrays. Sidney lights up a Wills' Whiff and starts making like Cecil Beady-eyes.

'It's the most satisfying thing I've ever done,' he says, nearly running an invalid car off the road, 'bringing culture to millions of people who haven't had my advantages. Being associated with so many great talents. Marvellous. It really is!'

He rambles on like this 'til we get there and I can sympathise with dad snorting and wheezing in the back. Sidney really can get up your bracket when he puts his mind to it.

I am a bit surprised that the bloke on the studio gates does not question us being there at this hour and even more so when I see a number of cars outside the hangar in which we have been shooting.

'They must be getting ready for tomorrow,' says Sid when I mention this to him. 'Don't let on that you don't belong or we'll have the union on our necks.'

'Don't you start being derivative about the unions, mate,' says dad. 'You wouldn't be where you are now if they hadn't established your rights.'

'I've never been in a union in my life and I don't intend to start now,' says Sid. 'I believe in Lassy fare.'

'That's a dog food, isn't it?' says mum. 'I've seen that on the tele.'

'Do belt up,' I say, swinging open the outside door. 'You are not really supposed to be here, remember?'

Once inside, I get another surprise. The lights round the set are on and there are a large number of people milling about.

'They must be doing a re-shoot,' says Sid. 'Look, mum, you'll find this interesting.'

Now, I don't know if 'interesting' is quite the word I would have used, but it is very difficult to think of a single word that adequately describes what is happening before our popping eyes.

Behind the camera is Justin Tymely and half a dozen naked girls are removing the clothing from a large black man. And when I say large, I mean large. This bloke obviously finished up all his runner beans when he was a little boy.

'Oh!' says mum.

'Oh, my God!' says Sidney.

Dad doesn't say anything. He has swallowed his dentures.

CHAPTER SEVEN

'I know, I know,' says Justin raising his hand. 'I know exactly how you feel. It was most unfortunate that you chose that moment to burst in on us. Of course I was going to explain all about Oliver NTwist.'

It is an hour after the remarkable revelation at the studio and we have saved dad's life – much to Sid's disgust – and sent him home with a bewildered mum. Justin is pouring generous slugs of scotch and explaining all.

'Oliver NTwist?' says Sidney.

'The Central African market is very big for us,' soothes Justin. 'They're not very well up in Dickens so we have to simplify the story line, give it a flavour that appeals locally.'

'You were making a blue movie,' accuses Sid.

'We call them Black and Blue movies,' says Justin in his best George Sanders voice. 'Listen, Sidney old bean. I feel I must explain one or two facts of life to you. The old motion picture industry in this country is a teeny weeny bit dicky, to put it mildly. Employing directors of Ken Loser's class costs a great deal of money. Your contribution, greatly appreciated as it is, covers only a fraction of your overheads. In a high-risk business such as this we have to take every opportunity to recoup our losses before they occur. Now. There is a guaranteed world market for films of – shall we say – a slightly risqué nature. By making these we can subsidise works of art such as the current Loser epic.'

'I didn't know I was putting up money for blue films,' says Sid.

'My dear Sidney. You are putting up money to finance a masterpiece. Put yourself in my shoes. Have I the right to put your money at risk when I can ensure a very healthy return for you *as well as* allowing you the satisfaction of participating in the creation of a work of art? There is a considerable amount of capital tied up in this studio and the equipment you see lying around. If we can utilise that twenty-four hours a day then we are maximising profits. You obviously look for a return on your money?'

'Of course, but I thought it would all come out of Oliver Twist.'

'It probably will but I feel it my duty to guard against disappointments. The public are very fickle. You can't guarantee success with purely artistic ventures in the same way that you can when you leaven the mixture with a trace of eroticism. By shooting Oliver Twist in the day and Oliver NTwist and Olivia Twist at night we double the profit potential.'

'What's Olivia Twist?'

'For the Swedish market. Again we've taken a few simple liberties with the original story line. We have replaced Fagin with the madam of a brothel – not Jewish of course, the anti-semitic aspects of the story have always been quick to give offence – and changed all the pickpockets to tarts.'

'I think it works better like that anyway,' says Sid. 'What was that you were saying about profit potential?'

'Very satisfactory. You could see a two hundred per-cent return on your investment. If we're shooting at night, of course.'

Sidney nods his head and I can see him racked by the conflict between artistic integrity and a few grubby green-backs. Eventually he draws himself up and utters the words that prove to me that when it comes to the crunch Sidney can be relied upon to act in a way consistent with the principles in which he believes so deeply.

'Can we shoot on Sundays?' he says.

'I think it's all very dicey,' I say to him later. 'Shooting with a non-union crew, flogging skin-flicks to Bongo Bongoland. It's a bit of a come-down, isn't it?'

'Don't you ever listen to anything anyone says?' chides Sid, who changes faster than litmus paper. 'You've got to make a few compromises these days. It's the end product that matters.'

'You mean the shekels you're going to rake in?'

'No! I mean the best Oliver yet.'

'I reckon you've got two of the best Twisters already. That man Justin is nothing more than a con man and Loser is a nutter. Have you seen any of the rushes of his stuff yet? It's junk.'

Sidney starts doing his pillar-box imitation. 'It hasn't been edited yet, has it?! No need to get all narky just because you haven't been made the bleeding star of the film.'

'All this sex and violence is played out, Sid. People want something light and cheerful.'

' "People want", "people want". People want shaking up, that's what they want. Remember what Loser said: "to vomit is to feel".'

'On the strength of what I've seen I'd say: "to see is to throw up".'

'You can sneer,' snarls Sid, 'but you wait 'til the film opens. Rave reviews and queues all round the Empire.'

'You mean the British Empire, do you Sid? Surely you're not thinking of Oliver NTwist. That should get them padding down to the chief's clearing.'

Sid's reply reveals that his nerve ends are fraying and in the weeks that follow, tempers all round the set become strained to the point of rupture. Glint's booze intake hits new heights and he only puts down the bottle to grab another hopeful starlet. Dawn Lovelost is also hitting the bottle and says that she is drinking to forget. Quite what, it is not very clear but those who have seen her before the camera suggest it is probably her lines. Loser's hysterical fits become more frequent and even Justin starts losing his cool and is heard to snap at the faithful Mac.

At last it is finished and I, for one, have no idea what the whole thing was about. I thought I knew the story of Oliver Twist and I never remember a bit when everyone wore gas masks and hit each other over the head with cucumbers. Nor the scene when Fagin takes Oliver to a brothel and every bed has an alligator in it. Most directors would have settled for dummies but Loser has to ransack a private zoo. Not only that but he has this bleeding great gorilla that moves up and down the corridor. I was dead choked because when I heard about the brothel sequence I thought I was going to be in like Flynn. But not a sausage. Loser did want somebody to get into bed with an alligator but I did not reckon it was my cup of tea. Even though the bleeding things were supposed to be under sedation they kept rolling off the beds and scuttling across the floor. Very unpleasant it was. One of them bit through a power cable and electrocuted itself and I wished it had been holding hands with its mates at the time.

The gorilla was no charmer either. It did take a fancy to Sid though and kept trying to stroke him. Naturally everybody used to ask Sid when they were getting hitched and this drove him mad. On one occasion I gave Charley – that was the gorilla's name – one of mum's bananas – you know, the brown ones – and it galloped across the set and shoved it in Sidney's cakehole. Didn't even take it out of the skin either. I tried to make Sidney see the funny side but his sense of humour deserts him sometimes.

With the film in the can the next thing to look forward to is the première and remembering Sid's words about the Empire, I am eager to find out where this world-shattering event is going to take place. I have always imagined myself wearing a white tuxedo and hot-knobbing with a bunch of Lea-crazy starlets. The flash-light flashing, the champagne corks popping. Then, the excited whisper going round the assembled throng as we form a line to curtsey to some regal personage: Lew Grade, Bernard Delfont, someone like that.

'The Bioscope,' says Sidney.

'The what?! Where's that?'

'Notting Hill Gate.'

'You're going to have the première there?'

'Justin says it's more fashionable to have your première out of the centre of London these days.'

'Oh, Justin says that does he? Well that must be all right then.'

'No need to get all narky,' says Sid menacingly. 'You don't have to come.'

'I'm not certain I'll be able to. Have you got a map of the area? I've never heard of the Bioscope.'

'It's an underground cinema.'

'Oh, it's in the underground, is it? Doesn't the noise of the trains –'

'Shut up! You know what I mean. It specialises in revolutionary cinema. Underground films. Wendy Arsehole, that kind of thing.'

'You mean Andy Warhol, you berk.'

'Him too. No need to get all worked up about it. I watch B.B.C.2 as well, you know.'

'Only Floodlit Rugby League. Oh, Sidney, I can't believe it. This blooming great cultural masterpiece creeping on at the Bioscope, Notting Hill Gate.'

'Don't knock it! Ken thinks that it's exactly right for the film. He doesn't want it to go in to one of those big, flashy places where they clean the wash basins and the pile on the carpet tickles your tonk. He says this is people's cinema.'

'Well, I hope he's right. I hear we haven't got anyone to distribute it yet?'

'They're just hanging on for the reviews. There shouldn't be any problem. Not with Loser's name attached to it. I'm expecting a couple of the big boys to come to the première. I reckon they'll be impressed.'

'Talking about who's coming to the première, Sid, what about mum and dad?'

'Yeah, I thought about that too. I can't see your old man in a dinner-jacket somehow. Now a strait-jacket. I can see him in one of those all right.'

'It would break mum's heart if she didn't come.'

'Yeah, I know. I'll invite them and hope dad doesn't show up. Once we mention he's got to wear a dinner-jacket that should put him right off.'

But it does not put dad off. Though he shakes his head and says 'Notting Hill Gate! I thought we'd given them their independence years ago.' I can see him filing the date away in his evil little mind; fully intending to put in an appearance.

The night in question is dark and drizzly and instead of searchlights sawing the air there is the fluorescent light from the 'Sixteen machine – no waiting, 24-hour-a-day Laundromat' next to the Bioscope, which seems to be drawing a slightly larger crowd than our première.

Sid and I stand next to the pay box, or in the foyer as Sid chooses to call it, waiting with Justin to receive the guests. I notice that some of the fat, elderly men who were at the casting session are also present. This time accompanied by plump, furry women with hair that looks as if it has been stuck together with Araldite and then sprinkled with Christmas-tree glitter.

'Oh, my Gawd,' says Sidney. 'Take a butchers at that.' I follow his eyes and see dad who is approaching us dressed in morning suit and top hat.

'At least he's left his binoculars at home,' I say but Sid is in no mood for jokes.

'It's diabolical,' he says. 'He's trying to make a laughing stock of me, I'll swear it. Did you ever see anything like it?'

'Now that you come to mention it, Sid,' I say, 'Yes. I have. Cop a load of mum.'

Yes, Mrs Lea has not been left behind in the smutter department. She looks like a cross between a pearly queen and one of those daft birds you see photographs of on Ladies' Day at Ascot.

'Blimey, I've never seen so much jewellery on anybody,' says Sid. 'She looks like a mobile junk shop.'

'Yoo hoo,' hollers mum, as I try and hide behind Sidney who is trying to hide behind me. 'Ooh, but we did have a lot of trouble finding this place. My feet are killing me. We had to stand on the bus.'

'I've got a diabolical crick in my neck,' grumbles dad. 'Standing downstairs with one of these hats on. I was bent double.'

'Why didn't you take it off?' I ask.

'He couldn't, dear,' explains mum. 'It was a bit big so

we had to wedge it on with pieces of newspaper.'

'I hope it was the Sporting Chronicle,' snarls Sid. 'Whatever made you put that lot on?'

'We both wanted to look nice for your film,' says Ma indignantly. 'Don't start having a go. If you knew the trouble I had to get him to wear something nice.'

'He looks smashing, ma,' I say hurriedly. 'You both do. Don't you reckon, Sid?'

Sid swallows hard. 'I wouldn't have believed it if I hadn't seen it with my own eyes,' he says.

'Let me introduce you to one or two people.'

Even Justin looks a bit taken aback when he meets dad, but under the influence of a few stiff scotches which are being dispensed from the pay desk, I begin to feel much more relaxed. Dawn Lovelost rolls up but does not get out of her car because not enough people have arrived. She has departed to drive round the block a few times when Glint Thrust appears supported by two incredible blonde birds with legs going up to their armpits and smiles as wide as water melon segments. When I say supported, I mean held off the ground. Glint is so stoned he staggers into the Laundromat and tries to check his cloak in to one of the washing machines. He slumps down in a chair and is only just prevented from knocking back a beaker of detergent powder.

Sandra Virgin's knockers are the next stars to arrive closely followed by their proud owner and a ripple of anticipation runs through her self-supporting bra as she bends down to kiss Mr. Guttman, the geezer who caught Sid on the job with his 'daughter'. That lady is nowhere to be seen but Samantha is tripping about, dropping people's coats and spilling drinks like she has been doing it all her life, which she has. She informs me that there is going to be a post-première party at Justin's flat where we will be able to wait for the first newspaper reviews to arrive. 'I hope you're coming,' she burbles. 'It's usually most tremendous fun.'

'Wild whores will not be able to drag me away,' I say, favouring her with a touch of the wit which has earned me the title of Clapham's answer to Noel Coward. Sam nods without smiling and goes on her way. I think she finds my brand of sophistication a bit overwhelming.

Now, at last, Dawn decides to honour us with her presence. Unfortunately it is now raining quite hard and in her anxiety to get into the cinema she manages to slam her stole in the car door. She takes one regal stride forward with the word 'Darling!' framed on her lips and then spins round as if brought up short in an apache dance. There is a loud ripping noise and she sits down in the gutter. Glint leads the cheering from the Laundromat where he has now persuaded a few people to ask him for his autograph. We rush forward to pick her up and it is obvious that she has knocked back more than a few shots of nerve tonic before venturing out.

'Terribly bad luck about the weather,' sighs Justin. 'I think it's keeping people away.'

Whatever the reason, there are certainly not a lot of people present apart from those appearing in the film and their next of kin.

'Do you recognise any film critics?' I ask Sid.

'No. But Justin says the bloke who does the Women's Institute Round-up for the Kensington Clarion is here.'

'That's blooming marvellous, isn't it? We won't be looking back, now.'

'Don't be sarky, Timmy. It doesn't suit you. The critics are probably here incontinent.'

'I think you mean incognito, Sid. Incontinent means you piss all over everything. Still that's probably what the critics will be doing, isn't it?'

Sid does not answer that but gives the word for me to start herding people into the cinema.

'What about Loser?' I ask.

'We can't wait any longer. They've nearly finished up all the booze.' This is certainly true and there is no doubt that, whatever you may think of the acting profession, they can say goodbye to a few bottles of the hard stuff so fast that you can hardly see their lips move. In this respect dad is not far from being their equal, and he is in excellent spirits as I shepherd him towards the door.

'Cor,' he says. 'Lucky I had your mother with me, the way some of these women are flaunting themselves they're asking for trouble.'

'They couldn't ask a better bloke, eh, dad?'

'I'm not saying anything about that, but I reckon if I played my cards right, know what I mean?'

'Be your age, father,' says mum sternly. 'Don't let's have no embarrassment at Sidney's primula. Ooh, I am looking forward to seeing you act, Timmy.'

'Well, don't drop your choc ice, or you'll miss it.'

'My grandmother was an opera singer, you know. I think it runs in the family.'

'She had such a lousy voice she had to run,' chips in dad.

'Shut your mouth!' snaps mum. 'You don't know what you're talking about. You never met her. It's no accident that Timmy and Jason came along.'

'What do you mean?' bellows dad. 'That's exactly what it was. Timmy was practically singing at our bleeding wedding!'

'I didn't mean like that!' says mum, turning scarlet. 'I was talking about their talent. That's inherited.'

'Yeah. Well, my lot weren't stupid, you know.'

'Mum! Dad! Please! Remember what you said. Don't let's have a punch-up at a moment like this.'

'The very idea. Going on like that. Just because Sidney and Rosie were so in love –'

'Yes, mum,' I say hurriedly. 'Where is Rosie? I suppose she is coming?'

There is no need of an answer to that question because I glance behind me and get an eyeful of the lady herself. Eyeful! By the cringe. I have not seen so much of Rosie since we shared the same bath tub as kids. Her dress is topless, backless and sideless, and it is amazing how the various parts of it succeed in meeting at all. Even the puff sleeves have slits in them and the whole outfit has more cuts in it than a pre-election budget speech. The long skirt is no more than strips of venetian blind hung verti-

cally and the blouse has air vents all down the fuselage.
The whole outfit looks like a cotton skeleton.

'Blimey!' I say. 'And in virginal white, too.'

'Do you like it?' says Rosie. 'You don't think it's too
much?'

'Quite the reverse, Rosie. What do you think of it,
mum?'

'It's very nice, dear. A bit – well – you know – sort of –'

'Diabolical?'

'Oh, no, dear. I wouldn't say that.'

'I would,' says dad. 'I'm ashamed to see a daughter of
mine degrading herself like that. You're making a proper
exhibition of yourself. You don't want to show all you've
got to a load of complete strangers!'

'Oh, you're so out of touch, dad,' spouts Rosie, adjusting the top of her dress against the weal mark that runs
through her nipples. 'This is a film première, isn't it?
You're supposed to dress up a bit.'

'"Up" is the word, my girl,' snorts dad. 'I've made an
effort to meet the standard required. I wouldn't have you
wear that thing to pop out to the kasi.'

'Because you're so stupid, that's why. The human body
is nothing to be ashamed of – though I can understand
where you got the idea from. These days you dress to
accentuate the body, not hide it.'

'No need to use words like that,' says dad. 'Speak language people can understand.'

'Rosie! Oh, my Gawd!' Sidney appears looking
harrassed. 'What happened? Did you go through the
automatic car wash?'

'Don't you start!' Rosie's lip is starting to tremble.

'I think it's like one of those costumes they wore on
Henry VIII on the tele,' says mum soothingly.

'Yeah. Henry VIII's. It looks better on a fella. Oh, my
Gawd. What have I done to deserve it? Still, never mind,
let's get inside before we miss the start of the film. You
look after mum and dad, Timmo.'

I am not overchuffed to hear Sid say that because dad is
a dead liability in any place of public entertainment. He

starts off by saying he wants to go to the toilet and by the time we get inside the cinema the lights have gone down and we have to feel our way to our seats. 'Feel' is the right word. Dad has his hands on every pair of knockers in the row and there are nearly some nasty incidents. 'They shouldn't wear dresses like that if they're frightened of somebody brushing against them,' he says. 'They're asking for trouble.'

'Sit down, dad,' I tell him. 'The seat folds down, you know that.'

Dad's habit of perching on a tipped up seat can get on your nerves after a bit.

'I can see better up here.'

'Sit down!' hiss the voices from behind.

'Belt up!' bellows dad. 'I paid for this seat, didn't I?'

'NO!'

'Shurrup!'

I haul him down and after a few minutes rabbiting he begins to concentrate on the screen.

'Oh,' he says, all surprised. 'You've got her in it, have you?'

'Who, dad?'

'Her. The Queen Mother. I thought I hadn't seen her opening anything lately.'

'This is the Pathetic News, dad. It's not the film!' Really, he is a stupid old berk, isn't he? When you spend some time with him you can understand what an uphill struggle people like Ken Loser have to bring culture to the masses. And where is Ken? It is surprising that he is not here for the première of his masterpiece.

No sooner has the thought bundled into my nut than the swing doors at the back of the theatre burst open and a white horse gallops down the aisle throwing its rider through the screen. The lights go up immediately and as the horse disappears through the exit marked gents, we see our Ken staggering back into the auditorium. He is wearing a fur hat, scarlet tunic and leather boots.

'He thinks he's a hassock, does he?' says dad.

'A cossack, dad,' I tell him. 'For Gawd's sake, don't you know anything?'

'Some kind of circus act before the film, is it?'

'Something like that, dad.'

Loser makes a big thing of embracing two birds and a bloke, and slumps down dramatically in a seat which collapses.

'It's not his lucky day, is it?' says dad.

'Ssh. The film is starting.'

'I want to go to the toilet again,' says dad.

I know I should go with the miserable old twit but I want to see what the audience's reaction is to the film. Justin has said that you can tell after the first ten minutes whether you have got a hit on your hands.

For five minutes I squint sideways into the gloom and the bloke on my left begins to nod off. This can't be good. I am looking around for a more favourable reaction when it occurs to me that dad should be back by now. What has happened to the silly old bugger? I push past the irritated whispers and go out into the foyer. Dad is standing by the pay box draining a glass.

'Just helping clear up the empties,' he says guiltily.

'Helping yourself,' I accuse. 'You've been polishing off the left-overs, haven't you?'

'It didn't take me long,' says dad, belching loudly. 'Didn't think it would, with your precious brother-in-law laying on the booze. That's just what he does. He lays on it so nobody else can get any.'

'Don't be bleeding ungrateful, dad. You've never risked rupturing yourself when it came to lashing out on entertainment. I remember you trying to raffle the cake at Rosie's wedding.'

'I was only thinking of raising a few bob for their honeymoon. They weren't going to eat it all, were they?'

'Whatever happened to the money, then?'

'Well. They left in such a rush, didn't they? I never got a chance to give it to them. Then, your Uncle Raymond came along and suggested we had a few. You know what he's like.'

'Yeah, I remember dad. Mum didn't see you for three days, did she? They reckoned you'd gone on the honeymoon.'

'Don't bring that up now,' whines dad. 'How much longer is there? I get chlorophyll in that place.'

'We should be so lucky, dad. You mean claustrophobia. Blimey, it's a good job I know what you're on about, isn't it? Hey, what have you got there?' Dad is trying to slip a bottle under the jacket of his morning suit.

'I found it lying in the pay box. I thought someone might nick it.' The thieving old git is only trying to stash away a bottle of scotch.

'Very commendable, dad. Now, hand it over.'

'Let's just have a little drink first, eh?' Dad gives a nudge and a giggle and I can see the signs that he is on the way. I should be firm but, on the other hand, maybe he will drop off if he has enough booze inside him. He has been known to pass out with his face in an ashtray on more than one occasion.

'All right, dad, but make it a quick one.'

Well, it is quick all right. Like emptying a bucket of water down his throat. The morning suit soaks up more scotch than he does. They should like that when he takes it back.

'Dad, are you sure you want to go back in there? Maybe –'

'No, son. I want to see what your precious Sid has been up to. Anyway, I like the royal family.'

'Their bit has finished,' I humour him. 'Now, give me that –' But dad twists away and takes another swig of scotch before we get through the swing doors.

'It's dark, isn't it?' he says loudly and resentfully. 'They don't make it easy for you, do they?'

'Quiet, dad! People are trying to watch the film.'

On the screen Glint Thrust is slapping Dawn round the kisser with obvious relish and the sight is not lost on dad.

'Hey, look at that!' he bawls. 'That's not nice, is it? Clobbering a woman. I don't hold with that.'

118

'Well, piss off then!' hisses a voice from the darkness. Dad does not warm to the suggestion.

'You want to watch your language, mate. You'll find yourself picking your teeth out of your hooter.'

'Shut up, dad. Get a grip on yourself.'

'They want to get a grip on themselves!' Dad points towards the screen and lurches into a row of seats. 'Look at it! Look at it! It's disgusting!'

'Oh! Keep your hands to yourself!' screams a female voice.

'You want to dress up then,' says dad. 'A bloke can't move around here without bumping into your flesh. You trying to inflame people, are you?'

'It's the second time he's done it, Siggy. You've got to do something.'

'You looking for a bunch of fives, are you?'

'Sit down!'

'How dare you touch my wife.'

'I know. It does take a bit of courage, doesn't it?'

'Oh!!'

'Sit down!'

'Shut your trap!'

'I'm sorry, I'm sorry,' I burble. 'He's a bit overtired. He's not himself.' This, of course, is a complete load of cobblers. Dad is behaving exactly like himself. Why the hell did we ever invite the miserable old sod? I try to drag him towards some empty seats but he waves his scotch bottle expansively and succeeds in sprinkling everybody within three rows.

'Shut up and watch the film, dad,' I hiss tearing the bottle away from him. 'You're not having any more of this 'til it's finished.'

'How can I have some when it's finished?' moans dad all heartbroken. 'That's not possible. You're not playing the white man with me.'

'When the film is finished,' I hiss through gritted teeth. 'Now belt up!'

But there is still a lot of life left in dad. On the screen Glint is now tucking into Dawn like she is a flaky meringue and I can see dad's evil little eyes gleaming in the darkness.

'Cor,' he grunts. 'That's not nice, is it? And on the kitchen table too.'

'It's not the kitchen table. It's a tavern.'

'I don't care what it is. It's disgusting.' And before I can stop him, dad leaps to his feet and starts chanting, 'What a load of rubbish! What a load of rubbish!' I should have guessed that all those evenings curled up in front of 'Match of the Day' would have an effect on him. The violence of the terraces has seeped into his miserable old ratbag body and has at last found an outlet. 'Off! Off! Off!' he bellows and hurls his empty scotch-bottle at the screen.

The audience has not been quiet since dad re-entered the cinema and now the noise takes on uproar proportions. To my surprise a lot of it supports dad's point of view.

'You took the words right out of my ball point,' exclaims a bloke in front of us before sloping out of the cinema.

'Hear, hear!' chant others. 'What a load of rubbish.'

Needless to say the reaction from the posh seats is of a different nature.

'Evict that enemy of the people's culture!' hurls Loser, sprinting up the aisle.

'Shut him up! Shut him up!' screeches Sidney desperately. 'The whole of my future is tied up in this film.'

'Quite a lot of your past too, I should reckon,' hisses dad. 'It's disgusting. Filthy!'

'Get this capitalist pawn out of the cinema!' yells Loser.

'"Porn". That's good, coming from you.'

'Sit down!'

'Shurrup!'

'Leave him alone!'

'Help, help. You'd assault an old man, would you? Help.'

'Assault him? I'll swing for him!' Sidney starts to push down the aisle towards us and for a moment I can see myself in the ridiculous position of having to defend dad against the thumping he so richly deserves. At that moment the screen suddenly goes blurred and a picture like molten lava running down the side of a volcano, appears on the screen. Apparently the projector has over-heated and the film is melting away before our eyes.

As if that was not enough, Loser's horse, having finished its business in the gents, or not having been able to push down the bar on the exit doors, comes racing into the audi-torium again. It obviously does not go to the cinema very often and, taking fright at what is happening on the screen, proceeds to race round and round the theatre, occasionally veering off up the central aisle for a bit of variety.

'Gee, I've been to some premières in my time,' says the guy cowering next to me, 'but this caps everything. You limeys really are getting with the razz-ma-tazz, aren't you? This is more like a happening than a movie.'

As if to prove the point Loser climbs up onto the organ seat at the front of the theatre and hurls himself onto the horse's back as it careers past. To the loudest cheers of the evening he then gallops up the aisle and disappears into the night through the exit doors.

'Gee. What a switch,' says the guy next to me. 'I can never remember a film ending with the director riding away into the sunset.'

'Or Ladbroke Grove,' murmurs Justin. 'Now, ladies and gentlemen, please don't leave your seats. We seem to have had a slight technical hitch but I'm certain we'll be able to continue showing this absorbing motion picture in just a few minutes. Thank you so much for your for-bearance.'

He sits down and the comparative silence makes me wonder what has happened to dad. I look down and there is the miserable old bleeder stretched out between a row of seats snoring away like the pig he is.

'Out like a light,' says Sidney. 'By the cringe, but I wish I could do something about making it permanent.'

'Is he all right?' says mum pushing her way to our side.

'Yeah, don't worry, mum.'

'I'm not worried!' Mum sounds as if she means it. 'I don't want him causing any more trouble, that's all.'

'He's so uncouth, isn't he?' sighs Rosie. 'He lets the tone down everywhere he goes.'

'Belt up and tuck your tits in,' snorts Sid. 'You're a fine one to talk about tone. The only Tone you know is the bloke behind the bar at the Highwayman.'

'Do give over,' says mum settling down and resting her feet on dad's body. 'I want to see the rest of this film. I think it's quite nice, really.'

But mum does not see the rest of the film because the projector refuses to work and Justin has to bound to his feet again and tell the fast-disappearing audience that he hopes they will see the complete movie when it comes to their local cinema.

'The week that rubbish comes to our local cinema is the week before the place opens as a bingo hall,' says one dissatisfied guest grimly. 'I always thought Loser was a vastly overrated talent and this junk proves it.'

'I expect Ken will join us at the flat,' says Justin evenly as the last of the outsiders disappears through the swing doors. 'Er – I was wondering what we should do about your father, Timothy?'

Dad is still stretched out in the middle of the theatre.

'Is this place well insured against fire?' asks Sidney.

'It's not well insured against what's happened out by the gents,' says the cinema manager who has been jigging about like a prat on hot pricks ever since we arrived. 'It's difficult enough getting the staff at the best of times without asking them to clear up things like that.'

'I'm very sorry,' soothes Justin. 'I'll speak to Mr. Loser about it.'

'It's his horse you should speak to.'

'Exactly, exactly. Timothy, I wonder if you would do me the most tremendous favour.

By the time I have finished doing Justin his favour and washed my hands, everybody else has pushed off to Justin's flat and I am left to struggle after them by myself. I have been looking forward to this particular knees-up for the last few days but after the events of the evening a lot of my enthusiasm has faded.

It is not replaced when I push open the door of Justin's swish apartment and observe dad through a glass darkly.

'How the hell did he get here?' I ask Sidney, who is standing a darn sight closer to Sandra's nipples than she is.

'He followed us in a tashi – I mean taxi,' stutters my stoned brother-in-law. 'Have you met thish lovely girl becaush you're not going to. You're far too nishe for him, aren't you, darling?'

I leave them to become better acquainted and notice that Glint is chatting up Rosie, his finger lightly running up and down her naked arms with the kind of scarcely restrained excitement he normally reserves for the neck of a whisky bottle. Oh well, good luck to them. I've done my bit to protect Sidney. I'm darned if I'm going to do any more. It is about time I started looking out for number one.

'Hello Timmy. I thought you were awfully good.'

'Thanks, Sam. I hardly noticed myself.' This is true. In all the confusion, God's gift to the British film industry got less than my usual quota of enthralled attention. 'Still busy are you?'

Samantha shakes her head slowly. 'No, thank goodness. I've been on the go from six o'clock this morning but I think I can relax now. They all look as if they think they're capable of looking after themselves, don't they?'

This is very true and an atmosphere of what you might call uninhibited gaiety prevails. It is a mood I must try and make the most of.

'I can never understand,' I say gazing into her mince-pies, 'why you haven't been snapped up by Justin or some other producer. You have a sweet, unspoilt quality that I find it difficult to put my finger on.'

'Not for lack of trying though,' says Samantha, removing my hand. 'Just because I was weak once it doesn't mean that I'm going to be at your beck and call. I've hardly seen you since that time we had lunch with your brother-in-law.'

'I know. It just shows you how hard I've been working, doesn't it? And if it isn't me it's you. It's difficult to find the time, isn't it?'

I return my hand to its original resting place and this time there is no impulse to remove it.

'You wanted to see me again, did you?' she says uncertainly.

'Of course I did. I've been looking forward to this evening for a long time because I hoped it would give us a chance to be together again.'

It's awful isn't it? But sometimes I don't think it matters what you say as long as you both want something to happen.

'Oh, Timmy. That is nice.' She turns her face up expectantly and I do not disappoint her. A gentle kiss to begin with and a firm squeeze of the hand.

'Do you know your way round this place?'

'What do you mean?'

'Well, it would be nice to find somewhere a little quieter to get reacquainted.' I give her another kiss and start moving my hand in an anti-clockwise motion over her bottom – you can use a clockwise motion if you like, nothing is going to drop off.

'Oh, Timmy, you are naughty.'

'I can't help myself. With you looking like that I haven't got a chance. Come on, Sam.' I take her by the hand and draw her down the corridor before she can say anything.

'I'm so weak,' she murmurs.

Smashing! I think to myself. If I don't get across this one in two shakes of a donkey's dongler then Tarzan wears a truss. I push her back into the first bedroom I come across and feel hopefully for a key. There isn't one but you can't have everything.

'Oh, Timmy,' she says. 'I do like you.'

That makes two of us, I think as I slip my hands underneath her dress. She makes a yum, yum noise and chews at my lips like she is trying to untie a reef knot with her teeth. Boy! With the effect I have on women I should start taking ugly-pills.

'You're wearing knicks tonight.'

'It's cold.'

'Doesn't feel cold to me.'

'Oh, Timmy, that's lovely.'

The next few minutes could be lovely for everybody but suddenly I hear a familiar voice outside the door.

'Come in here,' it whispers conspiratorially. 'I want to show you something.'

Dad! What the hell does he want? I have a good mind to tell him to piss off but a mixture of curiosity and modesty gets the better of me.

'Somebody's coming,' I say unnecessarily. 'Get in that wardrobe.'

Samantha does not seem over-enthusiastic about the idea but I push her into a jungle of Justin's trendy threads and bundle in after her. I pull the door to and it clicks shut.

'U-u-u-m,' murmurs Samantha, losing no time in getting cracking with her adventurous little pandies.

'Steady on! I don't fancy the smell of moth balls.' But once you switch on Samantha's ignition her engine starts revving up fit to blow a gasket.

''Ere, look what I've got!' Dad sounds as if he is right outside the door of the wardrobe. 'I bet you've never seen one like this before?' Oh dear! The mind boggles at what the dirty old sod is up to. What stupid scrubber can have got lumbered with him?

''Course I have. Is that all you brought me in here for?' No! That is my mum's voice. This is disgusting. Listening to my own mother and father rabbiting on in this vein makes me go hot and cold with embarrassment. What Samantha is doing to the front of my jeans does not help either.

'You've seen one shaped like this?'

'Of course I have. They're all shaped like that. Now put it away.' 'Yes, dad,' I breathe, 'Put it away, please!'

'You know how it works, do you? You pull this bit at the end.'

'Of course I know. Now come on. Are you going to play with it all night?' Mum sounds so matter of fact about the whole thing. I suppose this is the best way to humour him. Or maybe that is what twenty odd years of marriage does for you – very odd, some of them.

'Look, it goes red when I pull it.' Really!! Would that I could be in any other wardrobe in the whole of North London. It would make your flesh creep with a couple of strangers, but your own mum and dad! I find it disgusting even to think of them on the job, let alone having to endure this. 'I can't get it in now.' Dad's helpless whine sends fresh currents of nausea through my twitching frame.

'Oh, give it here! You're like a child, aren't you? I have to do everything. There, simple, isn't it?'

'Watch out! You've bent it.'

'Doesn't matter. Its still going to work. See? Still niffs the same, doesn't it?'

'Yeah. I'd better put it back.'

'Hurry up before somebody comes.'

I don't know whether it is because of a subconscious urge to stop this depravity or the fact that Samantha suddenly squeezes my moth balls, but my shoulder connects with the wardrobe door which swings open to reveal Percy pointing accusingly at my mum and dad. Dad has a large bottle of air freshener in his hand and one finger hooked in the wick control as if about to pull it like a hand grenade. Both he and mum are fully clothed.

'You filthy little devil!' explodes dad. 'What do you think you're doing?'

'Just slipping into something cool, dad.' I close the door swiftly as Samantha lunges towards me through the lightweights.

'What's he on about?' says mum.

'About every five minutes,' says dad. 'Come on, I feel like a drink.'

CHAPTER EIGHT

'What's a clitch?' says Sid.

'A what? Oh, a cliché. Something very corny.'

'Why don't they bleeding well say so, then? How are ordinary people supposed to understand words like that? I bet that's not an English word. How about "derivative"?'

It is a few days later and we are reading the reviews of 'Oliver Twist' that have appeared in the Sundays. They are not good. In fact they are diabolical. 'Sex for sex's sake.' 'Violence laid on with a trowel.' 'No concessions to artistic integrity.' 'I beg you to miss this film.' And those are some of the better headlines. Justin says that it is because the critics are jealous of Loser's genius and irritated by his off-hand manner but I reckon it is because he is a useless director. Sidney seems to be coming round to my point of view at last.

'He's too far ahead of his time,' mutters Justin.

'Like Martin Peters,' I say helpfully.

'More like Mary Peters,' snarls Sidney. 'I've always had my doubts about that bloke. His bloody chauffeur and those dogs. He wants to change his sheepskin and get his hair shorn.'

'Sidney! Now, come on. I always thought you believed the sun shone out of his light meter.'

'I'm not one to start casting nasturtiums while the enterprise is still under way,' says Sid loftily, 'but I think I can speak freely now. I didn't expect to make any moola out of a straight version of the movie but I did think somebody would find something good to say about it. As a prestige production it's got less to recommend it than a long-distance spitting contest. How many of the circuits are distributing it?'

'Well, old bean, at this moment in time –' says Justin,

'None of them. Just as I thought,' snorts Sid. 'So I suppose we're going to soldier on at the Bioscope for another couple of days until we're pushed out by "Naughty Nudes of Nineteen hundred and Nine".' Justin picks up a pencil.

'What was that again? Edwardiana is terribly popular at the moment. You might have something there.'

'I haven't got anything *here* have I?' says Sid bitterly.

'My dear fellow,' says Justin, putting his arm round Sidney's shoulder, 'you mustn't be discouraged. We can't guarantee a coconut every time you throw a ball, you know. I'm certain that sooner or later you'll make a tickle. Not many backers make a packet on their first flutter.'

'What about Oliver Twist and that other skin-flick?'

'Yes. They should bring in a spot of bunce.'

Sidney's face darkens. ' "Should"!? I thought they were supposed to be cast-iron certainties.'

Justin shrugs and waves his head about in a gesture of non-committal agreement. 'The picture is rather black in the middle of Africa at the moment. They're getting very puritanical. No mini-skirts or bikinis. All tits under tarpaulin and no afro haircuts. They're trying to stamp out Western decadence.'

'What about Scandinavia?' I ask.

'The market seems to be approaching saturation. They're onto pigs at the moment, or perhaps I should say –'

'Yeah, yeah,' says Sid hurriedly. 'I don't recall any porkers in our masterpiece?'

'Tastes change so quickly,' explains Justin. 'It's terribly difficult to keep abreast in this business.'

'I'd have thought it would have been very easy,' I say. ' "Keep a breast" – get it?'

'Shut up!' says Sidney. 'I don't need any of your lousy jokes at a moment like this.' He turns on Justin. 'So, reading between the lines, what you're saying is that I'm going to be cleaned out?'

'Nothing of the sort, dear boy,' purrs Justin. 'I'm only counselling caution, that's all. In this business the stakes are high but the rewards are immense.'

'I seem to be tied to one of the high stakes,' moans Sidney, 'but I don't see any sign of the rewards.'

'As I said, you must have patience. I'm certain that if you back our next idea you'll make a fortune.'

'You told me I was going to make a fortune with this idea. Didn't he, Timmo?'

This puts me in a difficult position because Justin is the only film producer I know and I want to keep in his good books – his good films as well, should he ever make one. However, I do recall him making it very clear to Sidney that the skin-flick side of the business was likely to pull in a few swift bob.

Luckily at that moment the telephone rings and I have a couple of minutes to think of an answer I never need.

'Good heavens!' says Justin. 'How many? Mounted police? Are you sure you've got the right cinema? B-I-O-S-C-O-P-E? Yes. That's right. Goodness me. Very well, we'll be right over.' He put the receiver down. 'Amazing!'

'What is?'

'Apparently, there are queues all round the Bioscope. People are fighting to get in.'

'Blimey! And it's only half-past eleven. Get your skates on. This I've got to see.'

By the time we get there we have convinced ourselves that a cache of banknotes has been found in one of the seats or the place converted into a knocking shop, but there is no doubt about it. The sign outside the cinema states quite clearly: ' "Oliver Twist" – a Tymely Loser Production. Vicious! Degrading! Disgusting!' The queue that starts in Kensington High Street is filing past posters quoting the critics as saying, 'Pornographic Twaddle', 'The violence appalled me', 'The sex sickened me', 'Insults the intelligence of a retarded ten-year-old', 'Makes "Crossroads" seem like War and Peace', 'No thinking person should see it'.

'Brilliant, eh?' We turn round and there is Mac standing beside us, practically wagging his tail.

'Did you do this?' asks Sidney.

'It's the only thing I could do. I read through every single review and the only favourable comment in any of them was that the credits were well handled.'

'Ken sent them out to be done,' says Justin.

'I'm not surprised,' continues Mac. 'They were quite nice. Completely out of character with the rest of the movie. Anyway, when I read that lot I thought: I can't build a publicity campaign round the credits. I mean, they're over in twenty-five seconds and if we put them at the end nobody is going to wait that long to see who was responsible for what they were watching.'

'Good thinking, MacDonald,' nods Justin.

'Then it occurred to me that we had so many anti-superlatives –'

'Yer what?' says Sidney.

'People saying it was the worst instead of the best. I thought: there's a kind of distinction for you. People might like to tell their friends they'd seen what is supposed to be the worst film ever made. I mean, I bet you'd be interested in seeing the ugliest woman in the world?'

'Not very,' says Sid. 'I'm married to her.'

'Very satirical,' says Justin. 'Yes, I see what you mean. And that, harnessed to the sex and violence – or social realism, as we call it – has done the trick?'

'I remember you saying that people were fed up with sex and violence,' I say.

'It depends how you handle it. If it's done badly enough then it seems to be all right.'

'I think there's another reason for the success of the film,' says Mac. 'People distrust critics as a lot of phoney highbrows, so that if they say a film is a load of rubbish then the average man in the street reckons it must be just his cup of tea.'

'Mac, I don't know how I'm ever going to thank you for this,' gushes Justin. 'When I look at that queue of lugubrious, long-haired layabouts, idly flicking the flies away from the ends of their noses with their bicycle chains, a lump comes to my wallet.'

'It's nothing, J.T.,' says Mac modestly. 'Nothing that a

couple of thousand greenbacks couldn't more than adequately repay.'

'I wouldn't dream of sullying an act that so embodies the very essence of true friendship with anything so sordid as money,' says Justin, squeezing Mac's eager hand in both of his. 'Some deeds are beyond price.'

Mac looks as if he would like to discuss the matter further but he does not get the chance. A whiff of sheep-dip indicates that Ken Loser is standing by our side. His mood is exultant. He waves an expansive hand at the queue and spits down the front of Justin's raccoon reefer jacket. He does not mean anything by it, it is just the way he speaks when he is excited.

'Huh!' he snorts. 'One in the eye for the lackeys of the capitalist press who dared to sneer at my genius.'

'Yes,' says Sid, 'but –'

'Exactly,' Justin moves in fast to prevent damage. 'A wonderful achievement, Ken, brilliantly capitalised on by Mac here. Congratulations both of you. I think we may have tapped a gold-mine. Of course it's going to need careful handling. Something rather unusual in fact. Mac has had one or two very original ideas, which we must discuss when you have more time.'

'Certainly, certainly,' says Loser. 'Anything must be better than that attempt at cultural assassination,' he indicates the posters. 'It's almost touching, isn't it? Despite the heinous slanders of the fascist hyenas, they still come.'

'Long may it continue, Ken,' humours Justin. 'Now, may I suggest we repair to the local hostelry and imbibe a few swift jars to celebrate this latest assault on our bank manager's credulity? I'm afraid I seem to have left my wallet at home, but I'm certain that Mac –'

As it turns out the boozer selected by Justin is dead opposite the cinema queue and I can see Sidney's beady eyes clicking like cash registers as he keeps an accountant's eye on the suckers trudging past.

'Multiply that by thousands and you have the scene all over the country in a couple of weeks,' beams Justin. 'It's very fortunate that we have the whole of our talented team here today because it gives me a chance to raise another outstanding project that has been taxing our perfervid imaginations of late, eh, Ken?'

'Filming the conception and birth of a baby through the baby's eyes,' says Loser enthusiastically. 'You see, we start off with this shot of an enormous –'

'No, Ken! I wasn't referring to that,' says Justin, hurriedly. 'I meant the Horror Westerns.'

'Horror Westerns?' says Sid in his 'Worried, Clapham' voice.

'Low budget Horror Westerns,' says Mac, soothingly.

'It's a brilliant idea,' rabbits Justin. 'And you could be in on the ground floor of it. I mean, this thing,' he nods out of the window, 'is going to run and run. Your great grandchildren will be living off it. You've got to do something with the loot.'

'I think I'll put it in a Building Society,' says Sid.

'Very secure, of course, but hardly going to bring in the returns that I can guarantee with this latest venture. Consider it. What two subjects never pall? Horror movies and Westerns. Put them together and you must have a box office smasheroo. Imagine the scene, Glint Thrust –'

'Not him again.' I have heard that Glint and Rosie were up to their old tricks again at Justin's party. Sidney was not pleased.

'I've got him on a six picture contract. He's practically paying me for the privilege of working. Now, where was I? Oh yes. Glint glides into this ghost town, and when I say "ghost", I mean ghost. He pushes open the door of the saloon and there, behind the bar, is the hideous creature from the Black Lagoon, liberated by an underground nuclear explosion. Only one man in the world knows how to handle him.'

'Count Frankenstein?' says Sidney.

'Precisely,' says Justin. 'Brilliant, isn't it? This one must make us all a fortune. It's got everything. Horror, horses, sex, violence, the wide outdoors, all wrapped up in one bonanza package by the old maestro here.' He hugs Loser enthusiastically.

'And lots of social comment,' says Loser seriously. 'I want this film to say something. I see the monster as the embodiment of the struggling proletariat, rising up against the brutal forces of international capitalism as represented by Count Frankenstein. His predilection for orgies with novice nuns is symbolic of –'

'Wait a minute, wait a minute!' croaks Sid, 'you're talking as if this is all signed, sealed and delivered. I haven't agreed to anything yet.'

There is a long pause before Justin shakes his head solemnly.

'Quite right,' he says, and both Loser and Mac nod in agreement. 'Absolutely right. We were jumping the gun. I'm sorry. Now, let's have another drink and talk the whole proposition over in detail. Barman, five large brandies please.'

Two weeks later, I am sitting beside Sid on a plane bound for Nicosia, which I have been told is in Cyprus, which I believe is an island down the other end of the Mediterranean from the Costa del Chips.

'They got this thing off the ground quickly, didn't they?' says Sid.

'It's the jet engines that do it,' I tell him. 'Your stomach will catch up in a minute.'

'I don't mean the plane, you berk, I mean the film. They were out there recceing locations almost immediately, weren't they?'

'I reckon they had it all set up before you sunk all those brandies and started busking that cinema queue.'

'I didn't do that, did I?'

'Yes, Sid. And then, when that other poor sod started to do a soft shoe shuffle, you tried to shove his spoons up his hooter. "This is my queue! This is my queue!" That's what you kept shouting. I've never seen anything like it.'

'I do get a bit funny when I've had a few, Timmo. You should have looked after me.'

'Do me a favour. When I tried to stop you signing the contract you threatened to bash my nut in with the Doctor Barnado's box.'

'Oh my gawd!'

'Yes, Sidney. That evening did not reveal you in your best light.'

'Evening! But I was home with Rosie by lunch time.'

'That was the next day.'

'Oh my gawd!!! I thought she was a bit funny.'

In his sober moments Sidney has explained that we are going to Cyprus because Justin has cooked up a deal which makes it an all-time low in low budget movie production. I have thrown out the names of Spain and Yugoslavia but these apparently offer us nothing when compared to the simple fun-loving Cypriots.

'You see, they haven't been exploited,' says Sid. 'We're going to be the first.'

'Sounds great, Sidney.'

'It is, it is. With local camera crews and the price at which we can get extras, Justin reckons this is going to be one of the cheapest movies of all time. These guys work for nothing.'

This may be true because they certainly do not seem to work for money. When we get to Mexos, where the unit is supposed to be located, the men of the village are enjoying a spot of Egyptian P.T. outside the local coffee-shop, their eyes registering only a flicker of interest as they watch an old woman stagger down the dusty street beneath about half a ton of firewood.

'We should have got a taxi, Sidney,' I say. 'I didn't fancy sitting with all those chickens. Some of them got very frightened.'

'Don't worry. They'll be all right if you soak them overnight.' Sidney averts his eyes from the unsavoury sight of my trousers. 'I didn't know it was going to be market day, did I?'

'Nevertheless, Sidney, I'd have thought we'd got past the stage of travelling by bus. You must be rolling in it.'

'You look as if you've been rolling in it, and all,' says Sidney gleefully, never being able to resist a chance for coarse humour. 'It's all right going on like that but you can't afford to throw it about. Count the pennies and gather ye rosebuds while ye may, is what I always say.'

'Very quaint and commendable, Sidney, but I still think you could lash out a bit more on creature comforts. I mean, I don't fancy putting up in any of the doss-houses in this dump.'

'You're not going to. We're sleeping in tents.'

'Tents?'

'I told you this was a low budget picture. I suppose you thought you'd be lording it in the Nicosia Hilton?'

I don't bother to answer that because sometimes Sidney gets up my bracket so far he starts affecting my breathing.

We walk through the village which pongs like Ken Loser getting excited and sure enough there is a large tent pitched where the last mud structure gives way to a wide, flat plain.

'Why is it parked there?' I ask.

'So as to be near the shooting.'

'But we're not using this place as a set are we? It looks like a convalescent home for run-down mosquitoes.'

'I don't know,' Sidney sounds puzzled. 'I thought they were going to build a set with local labour.

'If that was the local labour outside the café, they didn't look as if they could separate a pack of bath cubes.'

'We'll ask Justin,' says Sidney, sounding more cheerful the minute his lips wrap round the reassuring syllables of the Maestro's name, 'he'll know what's happening.'

But when we peel back the flap of the tent stirring uneasily in the hot wind, it is not Justin that we see. Sprawled amongst a welter of beer-cans and empty bottles is the familiar figure of Mac.

'My God! This place smells like a cats' comfort station,' snorts Sidney. 'What the hell's been happening?'

The person best equipped to tell us is stirred into action by the toe of Sidney's boot. This item he seizes fondly before attempting to insert an arm up its owner's trouser leg.

'You jig, jig, quick, quick,' he murmurs without opening his eyes. 'Mac, Mac like Fatima.'

'She must have been a right old boot,' says Sid. 'Come on, Mac, wakey, wakey!'

'Say that again and I'll bash your face in! – Oh, it's you,' says our Scottish comrade, all in one distinctly unpleasant breath.

'None other,' says Sid. 'Where is everybody?' Mac sits up and shakes his head.

'They're out looking at locations. We had a bit of a party last night.'

'It looks very convivial,' says Sidney. 'When are we going to start shooting?'

'You have to be very careful with that word around here,' says Mac. 'There's a lot of unrest between the Turks and the Greeks. At any minute it could get very nasty.'

'The ones we saw looked under no strain,' says Sid. 'Are the locals Turks or Greeks?'

'I don't know. I can't tell the difference. The trouble is that they can. It's one of the reasons why we haven't been able to get any sets built. They won't co-operate. It's worse than the bloody unions back home.'

'Here we go, Sid. I hate to say "I told you so", but –'

'Shut up! What about the camera crew?'

'Some of them are here.'

'Some of them?'

'The others had to go back and tend the vines.'

'Oh my gawd! Have they ever seen a camera before?'

'It's difficult to tell. None of our equipment has got through customs yet.' Sidney's face is that of a man deeply disturbed.

'So what have you been doing for the last ten days?'

Mac holds up a bottle to see if there is any liquid left in it. 'Looking at locations and, and –'

'And getting stoned!' shrieks Sidney. 'This is diabolical. All this moola I'm laying out and there's nothing to show for it except a load of pissholes in the sand. Where's Loser? Where's the cast?'

'What day is it?' says Mac.

'Thursday.'

'Well, they were here on Tuesday night, or maybe it

136

was Wednesday. Yes, it must have been Tuesday because that was the night Justin auditioned the belly dancers.'

'Belly dancers? I thought this was supposed to be a horror film?'

'They were horrible, some of them. Awful. Great rolls of fat and gobbling Turkish Delight all the time. I was –'

'Stop it! Stop it!' howls Sid. 'This is ridiculous. Is everyone going mad? We're supposed to be making a film and I'm standing in a tent in the middle of the bleeding desert with nobody here and sod-all happening. Somebody's got to get a grip!'

There is a dramatic pause disturbed by the sound of a vehicle approaching, the note of its engine punctuated by multiple backfires.

'That must be them,' says Mac helpfully.

'There's enough of them, isn't there?' I say, giving the cauldron another little stir.

Indeed, the screams and shouts of drunken laughter are echoing from many throats, some of them widening out into a pair of bristols by the sound of it.

'Now I extend my hospitality,' says Justin's voice, full of the bogus enthusiasm I know so well.

'So soon after the last time? My friend, I congratulate you. He is a most frisky little fellow, is he not?' This voice is full of Eastern promise and as rich as honeycake. Further information about the condition of Justin's frisky little fellow is denied us because the man himself pushes into the tent and pulls up sharply when he sees Sidney. For a split second his cool skips a few degrees above freezing point, and then the smile bounds back onto his lips as if held by a piece of elastic round his neck.

'Sidney. Timothy. What a lovely surprise! I don't think you've met Abdul ben Krafti, our local Mukhtar and very good friend.'

'Not unless you used to wrestle under the name of Istan Bull,' says Sidney. 'I once had the pleasure at the Wimbledon Baths Hall.'

'I have never visited the bath in my life,' says Mr. Krafti, and few standing to windward of him would care to argue the point. He makes Ken Loser seem like a Lifebuoy advertisement. He is a large, fat man with a hair-brush moustache and clobber straight out of the illustrated New Testament my Aunt Nora gave me one Christmas, and which I changed for a copy of 'Advanced Sexual Techniques' two days later. Well, I was nine at the time.

'The Mukhtar is being tremendously helpful in getting us established,' burbles Justin. 'He really knows the lay of the land.'

And more than one of them, I would say, by the look of some of the crumpet that is beginning to straggle into the tent. Knock-out birds with long black hair and eyes as deep and dark as treacle wells. A bit on the B.C. side threads wise for my taste, but that seems to be the rule out here.

'We've got a bit of way to go though, haven't we?' says Sidney, allowing a slight edge to creep into his voice.

'Mr. Nogget here has a hefty stake in the financing of the picture, so we have to be very nice to him,' says Justin meaningfully, nudging Abdul with his eyes. Mr. Krafti bows respectfully.

'He who holds purse strings enmeshes fingers deep in short and curlies. Jolly good fun.'

'Abdul performed Trojan service on our behalf during the war. Stoker ben Krafti I believe it was, eh?'

'Senior service, not Trojan service,' corrects Abdul. 'Yes, I served under the old red duster, cor blimey. I know what the sailor boys like.' He rolls his eyes and smacks the rump of one of the birds who is bending down to collect the bottles. Sidney coughs.

'Very interesting, Mucker,' he observes, 'but how are we getting on with "Revenge of the Monster from the O.K. Corral"?'

'That's only a provisional title,' says Justin hurriedly. 'I'm certain we can do better.'

'Bugger me, I hope so,' says Abdul.

'I don't want to give offence, Ben,' says Sid, 'but where precisely do we stand at the moment?'

138

'You stand exactly forty-five metres due east of Bhirim Agrabad's millet store,' says Abdul helpfully.

'Relax, Sidney,' interposes Justin smoothly. 'Everything is under control. It hasn't all been wine, women and song, you know. It's very bad form in this country to refuse hospitality, so we've had to play along for a bit.' I wonder which bit, I think to myself. I would not say no to any of them.

'I understand that,' says Sidney. 'I don't want to offend the Mugger. We probably wouldn't be here if it wasn't for what him and his lot did during the war.'

'Cor blimey, yes,' says the Mukhtar.

'What worries me,' continues Sidney without pausing for breath, 'is the question of when we are going to start shooting.'

'Shooting. Yes, shooting.' Abdul nods vigorously and draws his fingers across his throat in a gesture that I find rather puzzling.

'Virtually immediately,' says Justin. 'We sorted out a marvellous location today.'

'Sort out! Bloody great sort out!' Abdul is doing more nodding.

'I've abandoned the idea of building sets. We can save money and time if we use a local village. Change the setting of the movie to the Mexico border and nobody is going to know the difference. I think we're going to make a killing.'

'Yes! Yes! You never say a truer word, matey,' exults Abdul, his eyes revolving like Catherine Wheels. 'Kill! Kill! Kill! We get the bastards this time.'

'Tremendous enthusiasm,' says Justin. 'That's what I like about the man. Loser is fascinated by him. He calls him Mr. Life Force.'

'They have a lot in common,' says Sid, his nostrils twitching. 'What about extras?'

'No trouble, matey,' says Abdul. 'I have all the extras you need. They been waiting for this moment for a long time.'

'You mean the film industry coming to Cyprus?'

Abdul waggles his head from side to side slowly. 'Something like that.'

'And the equipment?'

'Abdul has a friend in the Customs Office.'

'Yes,' says Abdul. 'He very good friend and he owe me a favour. I think he help us. Of course, I may have to give him a little present.'

'You mean bribery?' Sid looks unhappy; not because of the principle, but because it might cost him a few bob.

'It's going to save money in the long run,' says Justin. 'When in Rome . . .'

'When in Cyprus it costs twice as much,' murmurs Mac. 'He's a cunning bastard that Muhktar. There's no flies on him because they can't afford the rent.'

'The living conditions don't appeal to me much either,' I whisper. 'Tell me, what is a Muhktar?'

'Sort of head man. Squire of the village. He carries a lot of weight around here.'

'He carries a lot of weight around everywhere,' I observe, showing that the strong sunshine has not taken the edge off my rib-tickling wit.

'You must be parched after your journey,' says Justin, turning to us with a flourish. 'How about a spot of ouzo?'

'Well,' says Sidney, 'it's a bit public but I wouldn't say no. Which one did you have in mind?'

'I'd like the dark one with the big tits,' I say quickly.

'Gentlemen, please! You must excuse them, Abdul. Their high spirits get the better of them sometimes.' He turns back to me. 'I was referring to ouzo, the Cypriot aperitif.'

'I had an aperitif at that restaurant, didn't I?' says Sidney. 'I can't remember what it tasted like though.'

'Ouzo is rather like absinthe,' explains Justin. 'Surely you've heard of that?'

'Oh yes,' says Sidney, brightening. 'That's one of them afro drinks, isn't it? Makes you come over all fruity.'

'Absinthe an aphrodisiac? Not any more than any other alcoholic drink. What made you say that?'

140

'Well, there's that saying isn't there? Absinthe makes the heart grow fonder.'

'Oh my gawd!' You don't know whether to take him seriously sometimes, do you?

Before Sidney can cause any more suffering there is a scream from the other end of the tent where Glint Thrust is discovered dozing amongst a pile of sleeping bags. One of the bags in question has clearly taken exception to something Glint has said or done—more likely done. There is a brief flurry of activity and a half-naked girl shoots past pulling a shawl around her shoulders. I do not understand what she is saying but she is obviously not volunteering to be secretary of the Glint Thrust fan club.

In the circumstances it is difficult not to sympathise with Sidney and when Dawn Lovelost limps in supported by half a dozen local lustmongers, whose trousers are as tight as a gnat's foreskin and who give off a pong like the perfume counter in Woolworths, one can see his powers of self-control beginning to wilt like a nobbled nasty.

'What is this?' he groans, 'a film unit or a mobile knocking shop? Where have you been?'

'The boys have been showing me the local countryside,' giggles Dawn. 'Nice boys.'

'Showing you the bleeding sky, more likely,' snorts Sid. 'Brush the sand off your backside for gawd's sake. Now, where's blooming Loser got to?'

'I saw his camel,' says Justin.

'His what?!'

'His camel. Loser is a great man for cultural identification. He finds this particular locale brings out the Lawrence in him.'

'You're talking about Gertrude, of course,' sneers Sid. 'What a carry on! I've never met such a bunch of weirdos.'

At least Loser will have got out of his sheepskin coat, I think to myself and I am right. A scream of rage and pain, simultaneous with that of a heavy object striking the ground, suggest that K. L. is without. Without the ability to ride a camel, as it turns out. Lying on the ground wrapped in a large sheet, he looks like a pile of dirty washing waiting to take up the Daz challenge. His erstwhile mount bends its head low and sweeps it backwards and forwards across the ground like a respectful Geiger counter.

'Bloody brute,' yells Loser, scrambling to his feet. 'Capitalist lackey!' He swings his boot at the camel, misses, and sits down hard. 'Otto!'

Looking like a refugee from Beau Chumps, Otto limps round the corner of the tent.

'I said, walk a few paces behind me,' hisses Loser. 'Where the hell do you think you've been?'

'Oh, piss off, ducky,' sniffs Otto. 'I only took the job for the uniform, and now that's gone up the spout, you can as well. Good afternoon!'

He turns on his heel and minces off with Loser hobbling after him. 'Otto! Don't be so petulant. I'm sorry. I've been a bit overwrought lately. I didn't mean – Otto . . .'

They disappear towards the village and Justin shakes his head.

'Oh dear. I hope they patch it up. This could delay things a bit.'

It is one of the few times I can remember Sidney actually crying.

CHAPTER NINE

'It's quite large, isn't it?' says Sidney. 'More like a town really.'

It is three days after our arrival in Cyprus and we are waiting outside the village that Abdul suggested could take the place of a set. Loser and Otto are now friends again – or whatever they were before their tiff – and to prove it Otto is kitted out in white towelling Bermuda shorts and matching short-sleeved jacket with zip-up front.

'So cool and so chic, dear,' he chortles happily.

Abdul seems very chuffed about the location. 'This top-hole place for massacre,' he says. 'Cor blimey, yes.'

'Not "massacre" Abdul,' smiles Justin indulgently. 'We're going to shoot the peons riding into town for their confrontation with the monster.'

Abdul nods. 'Much shooting. Bang! Bang!' He waves cheerfully to the crowd of extras he has recruited and they shake their weapons enthusiastically.

'Pity about the donkeys,' says Sidney.

'In a way, yes,' says Justin, 'but it does add authenticity. And of course it saves money. This is a low budget movie, remember.'

'Yes,' says Sidney. 'I suppose if we're going to have donkeys instead of horses we might as well have dwarf actors to go with them. We could shoot all the scenes beside a doll's house.'

'Don't be like that, Sidney,' I chide. 'Look on the bright side. It's very fortunate that the Mugger's friends have all got their own guns, isn't it? That's going to save a few bob.'

'Yes,' says Sid. 'It's funny that. Abdul told me they kept them for shooting sparrows. I've never known anyone shoot a sparrow with a Browning sub-machine gun before.'

'Very unsporting,' says Justin.

'Very.'

There is no doubt that Abdul's friends are as mean a bunch of layabouts as I have ever seen pinned up on the notice board outside Balham Police Station. And armed to the back of the National Health dentures their in-laws have sent them from Blighty. Shot-guns, sten-guns, pistols, It looks more like Sicily than Cyprus.

'They're not loaded are they?' I ask Abdul nervously.

'They drink a little, yes, but only to keep the spirits up.'

'I meant the guns,' I say.

'Oh, them. No. Most of them are family heirlooms.' At that moment there is a loud report and a shot-gun blasts the olive branch above my head.

'Don't waste your ammunition!' screams Abdul. 'You are going to need every bullet.'

Something deep down inside is telling me that Abdul is not all he seems to be. I cannot put my finger on it exactly but I do not completely trust him. If you listen to him very carefully he does come over as a bit of an agro merchant. Maybe I should talk to someone about it. But, after all the delays and hang-ups I am hardly going to be very popular if I start tugging at Sidney's sleeve just as we are going to start shooting.

'It's lovely, isn't it?' Mac is waving his camera about and has been taking footage of the local scenery ever since we caught up with the unit. Unit. It just does not seem the right word for our bunch of ill-assorted lay-abouts. 'Just look at that church,' continues Mac, pointing towards the town. 'Bleeding beautiful.'

'The bells sound lovely too,' I say. 'Funny how they started ringing the minute we got here. I expect Abdul laid it on. It certainly gives atmosphere.'

Before we can discuss this fascinating point further, Ken Loser starts to address us from the camera jeep which is going to follow the riders into the town.

'O.K. Shut up, Scarci!' he bellows. 'I want to give you the motivation for this scene.'

'Oh no!' groans Sid. 'Every time we do anything, all this bleeding rabbit. What's the point? They're not going to understand a word he says.'

I think Sidney is right. Most of the extras are either on their knees facing towards the East or polishing their weapons.

'So you see, we equate the return of the monster with the second coming of Jesus Christ,' drones on Loser. 'You are wise men, the shepherds down from the hills, drawn as if by a magnet to an event which fuses nuances of the resurrection with a kind of spiritual Armageddon. It is the beginning, and at the same time, the end.'

'It's the bleeding end all right,' moans Sid. 'Why doesn't he just tell them to saddle up and ride like buggery. Anyhow, you'd better get out there, hadn't you, Timmo?'

I have been cast as one of the peons and it is not a role I relish. It is not a word I care for very much, either.

'Do I have to, Sidney?' I bleat. 'I feel such a berk on one of those donkeys. My feet drag along the ground on both sides.'

'Well, tuck them up then, and stop whining. Every time we give you a part you start squealing.'

'But I didn't want to be buried up to my neck in an anthill.'

'Oh belt up!'

I take my place with the local talent and observe that Abdul is translating Loser's instructions. At least, that is what I think he is doing. There is much pounding of fist against palm and the now familiar throat-cutting gesture.

'Just keep it rolling,' shouts Loser through his megaphone. 'Very gentle at first, then speed it up as the religious hysteria gets the better of you. I'll give you the time.'

'It's half-past one!' shouts Sidney. 'Let's get on with it. We've been here a week and –'

'Roll 'em!!'

No sooner has the first word escaped gratefully from Loser's lips than the riders on either side of me dig their heels into their mounts and disappear into a self-constructed dust storm, screaming like Sidney when he caught the tip of his tonk in his chest expander. We have been issued with sombreros to build up the Mexican atmosphere but unfortunately mine is too big. It drops over my eyes and by the time I can see again I am trotting off at right-angles to the rest of the riders. I pull my donkey's head round and concentrate on keeping my balance, my hat and my lance. This latter article is all that I have been issued with and I am a bit sick that even those Cypriots with two or three weapons have not been prepared to lend me one of them. I suppose they are frightened of getting them damaged. When you've had a sub-machine gun in the family for a few years you must get very attached to it.

I am about twenty yards behind the last rider, with Loser cursing me, when the first shot rings out. Saucy monkeys. I think to myself. Just like boy scouts having a frolic!

Bang! Something whistles past my hooter and there is a sharp report as one of the tyres on the jeep blows out. Clumsy sods! They should be more careful where they are discharging their weapons. I try to rein in my donkey but the miserable little brute has now got its ears flat against its head and is thundering along at almost ten miles an hour. The first house of the town looms up and — Bang! I distinctly see a man pointing a gun at me from one of the windows. What the hell is going on?! Has Loser rigged up some diabolical scheme to wring a spontaneous reaction from us? Bang! This time my hat is torn from my head and I know that someone is using real bullets. I am a naïve sort of berk and I still think that there has been some kind of terrible mistake. No one would want to shoot nice, friendly Timothy Lea, would they? Bang! Bang! Bang! Blimey! The answer must be YES!!

The last burst of shots coincides with our arrival in a large square and all around us I see puffs of smoke as we are fired upon from window and roof. Abdul and his men leap off their donkeys and run towards the buildings and I look for somewhere to take refuge. Not unnaturally per-

146

haps, my donkey has the same idea and bolts towards a narrow alley. I am all for this, but unfortunately my lance has worked its way into such a position that I am holding it across my body. The donkey disappears down the alley with its fat little flanks practically scraping the sides and I am left suspended in mid air for a couple of seconds before crashing to the ground.

I lie there wondering if I have broken my back and then the sound of angry shouts jerks me to my feet faster than you can say 'Lea for Coward of the Year'.

Three steps down the alley and there is a big, dark, inviting doorway. I whip through it and find myself at the bottom of some steps. No time to hang around. Up the steps and there is a handsome middle-aged bint sitting beside a table. She smiles and nods. 'You have come.'

I am in no position to argue with her and so return her nod. She waves me towards a chair and claps her hands. 'Coffee?'

I am concentrating on the stairs but coffee seems a very good idea. 'Er – yes. Thanks. Thanks very much.'

'English soldier?'

'Me? Oh no. No. I'm a – I'm here on holiday. Beautiful. Very beautiful.'

As if on cue a cracking looking bird comes in carrying a tray with a small cup of black coffee on it. I would have preferred something big and white but I can hardly be fussy in the circumstances. The bird appears to be wearing a silk dressing gown but I am not paying too much attention. It is probably some kind of national costume. I sip the coffee, which tastes as if someone has forgotten to add water, and smile nervously at the lady behind the desk who smiles back. They are obviously a very friendly people, the Cypriots – some of them. I do not wish to venture out into the less friendly streets for a while so I pick up a book of photographs which is lying beside my chair and browse through it. I reckon I must have stumbled into the local dentist and been mistaken for somebody with an appointment. The pictures in the book are very revealing and their like would vastly improve the appearance of any waiting-room back in the old country. I must have a word with the Minister of Health about it.

They are all of birds. About half a dozen of them, in a variety of poses fit to turn you on like the Blackpool illuminations. The lady behind the desk is looking at me again.

'Which one you like?' she says. A bit forward but in my present mood of quavering terror I have other things to concentrate on.

'Oh – er, all of them,' I squeak, still looking towards the stairs.

'All of them?!' She sounds surprised and says something in what I imagine is Greek.

But I am not really listening. Someone has come in through the doorway below and there is the heavy clump of boots approaching up the stairs. I don't mind about the boots, it is what is inside them that is scaring the jockey briefs off me. I jump to my feet and am running towards the verandah as Mac's head and shoulders come into view supporting his precious camera. He sees me, and we both come down to floor level at the same instant.

'My God, you terrified me,' he sobs. 'They're going mad out there. That maniac Abdul is trying to wipe out the whole town.'

'Ah, he is your friend?' nods the lady behind the desk looking at Mac as if a source of puzzlement has been removed. 'And you like all the girls.'

'Yes!' I snarl. Stupid old ratbag. Rabbiting on about crumpet while the streets are running red with blood.

'I must get some footage of this,' says Mac. 'If we ever get out of this alive I'll make a small fortune.' He moves on to the verandah.

'Hey! Where are you going?' I demand, but our lady friend has disappeared down a corridor. Maybe she has gone to give the alarm? I start after her and immediately my hooter is assailed by a delicious pong. It does not niff

148

like any dentist I have ever been to. I wonder what it can be?

'Hello, darling.' I am not talking to myself but being addressed by a lady with jumbo-sized knockers barely concealed behind a slip of exceedingly modest proportions. Without waiting for an introduction she entwines her arms round my neck and kisses me like it is a lip trip she has been saving up for all her life. She has emerged from a room containing a low bed and little else that readily catches the eye. Cyprus is a pretty island, I think to myself, but not a good place to come to if you are of an excitable disposition.

'Where is the greedy one?' As the first charmer draws me into her lair so another black-haired beauty appears and proceeds to interfere with my clothing.

'Ladies, please!' I gulp.

'The English have such lovely manners,' murmurs Girl Number One. 'They ask for things they have already got.'

'W-wait a minute,' I stammer. 'I've seen you before. And you. And you. And you. And you. And you. You were in that book, weren't you? Oh!' I say 'oh' because it suddenly occurs to me that I have taken refuge in nothing more nor less than an old Cypriot Knocking Shoppe. No wonder the bint in reception was asking me what bird I liked best. And I said, 'all of them'. Oh my gawd! I try to escape but the girls reckon I am being playful. Six of them. What the hell am I going to do with six pieces of Cypriot crackling? The answer, as it turns out, is: very little. These birds have everything under control.

'First, we bathe and anoint,' murmurs Queen Tits sensing my uncertainty. 'That is free in lieu of bulk discount.'

'No bulk discount?' I inquire.

'No. It demeans status of woman to be offered free as incentive bonus.'

'Of course.' You can't escape from the language of marketing these days, can you?

'And then we indulge in traditional Cypriot nibble fest.

'Three start at one end and three at the other and we meet at –'

'Yes,' I gulp. 'That sounds fantastic, but I'm afraid I've left my wallet at home. I won't be –'

'You make playful joke,' says the Eyeful Twoer. 'We all appreciate English sense of humour. Strong on understatement. But, no man would be foolish enough to order six girls if he could not pay for them. The consequences would be too severe.'

'I know, but –'

'Please. Not to interrupt. All our girls are most highly bred and have been taught that it is bad manners to speak with mouth full. Now, is your friend joining us for love ritual, or will he continue to record scene for posterity?' I thought the whirring noise was my fly buttons going into orbit but it is Mac making with the movie camera.

'Stop pointing that thing at my person,' I holler. 'Have you no decency?'

'All part of life's rich tapestry, old chap,' exults Mac. 'Could you ask the girl lying on your – yes, that's right dear – to move her – fine – a bit more over towards – excellent.'

I would like to get off the bed and biff him on the hooter, but I am powerless. I don't know if you have ever had half a dozen strapping birds clambering over you but it does cramp your style a bit. I would like to say that I shrugged them contemptuously aside and stalked out to complain to Lord Longford, but this is not the case. In such situations I have a very poor record of self-control, and I have seldom been exposed to such creative and generous exponents of the art of bedsnake bashing. Even with Mac steaming up his aperture I am soon being lulled into a world of sensation that makes me feel like an electrified paint palette with all the colours melting into each other. I care not that I am being observed and surrender myself to an appreciation of the skills handed down from generation to generation of Cypriot craftswomen. After a prolonged period of rhythmic group activity, Miss

Sinneramour Holiday climbs on top of me and I slip into her easier than a bad habit. Adjusting herself with great care she begins to rotate her pelvis and I close my eyes and wonder if I am being introduced to some kind of fleshly heaven.

When I open them again it is to wonder if I am making acquaintance with the other place. A column of smoke is rising past the narrow window and I can see tongues of flame and hear the crackle of burning wood. The town must be on fire. Mac stumbles back from the window where he has been taking pictures and shouts at me.

'Come on! We've got to get out of here.'

This sounds like a great idea, especially as the ladies have just taken me out of myself. 'I think he has a point there, which is more than I have at the moment,' I bleat. 'Let's call it half time and I'll drop in again next time I'm passing through. I reckon I could well be here for the Queen's Golden Wedding Anniversary celebrations.'

I try to sidle off the bed but the girls are not having any.

'You pay now,' says Big Tits menacingly, 'otherwise we keep little momento of your visit. The last man who did not pay is now one of Turkey's most promising sopranos.'

'Look on the bright side,' says Mac. 'You'll never need a vasectomy.'

His amusement at his crude attempt at humour is short-lived. 'You are in same boat,' says B.T. 'I want four thousand mils between you.'

I wish there were four thousand miles between us, but what can I do? 'I have an Access Card,' I say. 'It stops you waiting for what you want until you wilt because you can't.'

'Cash!!'

Typical! None of these bleeding things are any good when you really need them. And B.T. has just produced a curved dagger with a nasty looking notch in the end of it. It is definitely time to say 'bye, 'bye.

'Look at that rat!' I scream. 'The one with the big furry spider in its mouth!'

It may not seem like a brilliantly orginal idea but these

are not brilliantly original birds. Handy for the torso tangling but I bet they never see the tele or any other art-form which might lubricate their imaginations. They all start screaming and scrambling on to the bed and I am through their legs and heading for the verandah with Mac at my heels before you can say 'Mary Whitehouse for Prime Minister'. I throw one leg over the parapet and – yee-oow! That scorched wood is no balm to the old action man kit, especially after what is has been through in the last hour. I stand back and vault into the street, arriving seconds before Mac and the camera.

Immediately two figures in soldiers' uniforms run out of the smoke and one of them belts me over the head with a club.

'Take that, you heathen scum!' he exclaims in a broad Irish accent. 'Look at this degrading spectacle, Paddy. We're flushing out the real depravity now.' I gaze up and see that he has the letters U.N.O. stitched on his shoulder. These, I recall, stand for United Nations Organisation and indicate that he and his friends are stationed on the island to keep the peace between the Greeks and the Turks. He bashes me again.

'Doesn't it make you sick, Paddy. They're all savages, the lot of them. Flying at each other's throats the whole time. Why can't they live together in peace like normal decent people. It makes my heart bleed to be back in dear old Ireland.'

'My head is already bleeding,' I yelp. 'Do you mind not bashing me with that thing? My friend and I are over here making a film. We have had nothing to do with any local conflict.'

'It's a fine kind of film they've been making I think to myself, eh, Seamus?' says the second mick eyeing my naked, scented body suspiciously. 'Perverted, I'd say.'

'Definitely. The whole place is rotten as an old cheese. Shake it and all the maggots drop out.'

They nod wisely to each other while Madam and the girls come streaming up behind us.

'You don't happen to have four thousand mils on you,

do you?' I ask hurriedly. "I have an Access Card." I pat the part of my body where my hip pocket would be if I was wearing trousers, 'but I'm afraid that –'

'Thieves! Robbers! Assassins! Heaven be praised that you have caught them.'

'Arrest me,' I whine. 'Don't let them get me. They're not nice.' The mick's eyes are like those found in potatoes but they widen appreciably at the sight of the girls, most of whom have not bothered to put on more clothes than would be needed to cover a Kamikaze pilot's post-war credits.

'Skipped out without paying, did they?' says Seamus, showing evidence of under-employed grey matter. 'We'd better take down a few statements?'

'Definitely. Come on, ladies, get inside, please.' The protesting girls are prodded back into the brothel and Paddy is already loosening his belt as he follows them through the doorway.

'You couldn't throw down my trousers, could you?' I call after him but there is no answer.

'If you say anything more about your bleeding Access Card I'll swing for you,' says Mac. 'Let's get out of here before the whole place burns down.'

The sounds of shooting have died away and parts of the town are now blazing cheerfully as we walk down the street.

'Let me hold the camera,' I ask. 'Then I won't feel so naked.'

At the end of the street is a small square and in the middle of it a landrover bearing the insignia 'First Battalion – Celtic Rangers.' The driver looks me up and down with faint interest.

'Your mates are searching a brothel,' says Mac.

'I'd better help them,' says the driver. 'Look after this lot for me will you?'

'Third on the right,' I call after him.

'Trusting soul,' says Mac. 'He's even left the keys behind.'

'Handy if there's any danger of it catching fire and we want to move it.'

'Exactly.'

'Do you want to drive?'

'If you like.'

'Right. Let's go!!'

CHAPTER TEN

' "Third World War narrowly averted." That's nice, isn't it?' says Sidney. 'Did you realise that both Greece and Turkey were preparing to invade and that Russian missile carriers were moving out of the Black Sea?'

'I know the American Third Fleet cancelled its courtesy visit to the Cannes Film Festival. Mum saved all the papers.'

'And Ted Heath not going to the Boat Show. Blimey, it must have been serious.'

'And all because of blooming Justin Tymely and his mate Abdul.'

'I'm going to speak to Justin about that when I see him. I'm still getting letters from the United Nations about that landrover. Blimey. You'd think with all the money they've got they wouldn't start worrying about a little wear and tear on the way to the airport. I mean, what do you pay taxes for?'

'Exactly, Sid. I feel the same way about that bill from the Cyprus government for rebuilding the North East end of the island. It wasn't our fault the wind changed direction and they were having their driest summer for twenty-five years.'

'Anyone would think we started the fire. It's so unjust. I mean, I don't like to point the finger at someone behind their backs, but if anyone is to blame it must be Abdul. Just because he's now got his own late-night talk show on the tele doesn't mean he should be able to escape all responsibility. They're like royalty, these people.'

Sid and I are on our way to the première of 'Revenge of the Monster from the O.K. Corral'. We have seen little of Justin, Loser and the film crew since our hurried return to England, and shooting has apparently been taking place on Wanstead Marshes.

'Typical, isn't it?' says Sid sulkily. 'If they can shoot

the film on Wanstead Marshes now, why didn't they think of that in the first place. It's always the bleeding same with these people. They spend money like water.'

'The light isn't so good,' I tell him.

'They don't drink light. They're all on gin and whisky, aren't they?'

'Oh, give over, Sid. What I don't understand is why we've got the Empire Majestic for the première after all the trouble we had last time.'

'It's because they have to show a quota of British films every year and there is nothing else available at the moment. I believe they've had to move like stink to get the film ready.'

This impression is confirmed when we bump into Justin in the foyer.

'Cross your fingers, lieblings,' he breathes. 'The film only came out of the cutting room fifteen minutes ago. Nobody's seen it yet.'

'Blimey. What, none of it?'

'Well, I've seen one or two snippets. Of course, Cyprus is a bit different from Wanstead Marshes. The light –'

'Yes, we've been discussing that,' I say hurriedly. 'Tell me, who are those geezers wandering about over there?'

I am referring to a tall bloke with woolly hair who looks as if he goes around sniffing little girls' tricycle seats. He is accompanied by a woman wearing a tweed suit and hair that must have been cut with a pair of garden shears. There are also one or two other geezers with faces longer than an advertising executive's lunch hour.

'That's the Fight Unclean Culture Korps,' explains Justin.

'Blimey. I've seen their initials everywhere,' says Sidney. 'They're getting a lot of support, aren't they? What are they doing here?'

'A lot of small-minded people said that our Oliver was obscene,' says Justin. 'It's a ridiculous charge, of course, completely ignoring the intention behind Loser's work –'

'Yes, but what are they doing here? Also those blokes

in hob-nailed boots and badly fitting suits reading the Police Gazette?'

'Well,' says Justin, lowering his voice, 'if you promise not to alarm yourselves, I'll tell you. We've been tipped off that the police are going to arrest everybody if the Fight Unclean Culture Korps judges the film is obscene.'

'Right! Where's the nearest bus stop?' Sidney is speaking over his shoulder.

'Come back, Sidney! Relax, old chap,' beams Justin. 'We've made absolutely certain that there is nothing in the film that transgresses current ethical and aesthetic standards.'

'Yeah, but what about the filth?'

'I was referring to the "filth" as you so charmingly call it,' purrs Justin. 'The film is unequivocal but certainly not pornographic.'

'Oh,' says Sidney. 'Well, I suppose that's all right then. I don't fancy another – I mean, I don't like the thought of imprisonment.'

'Very understandable,' smiles Justin. 'Well, you must excuse me. There are one or two rather influential people I must talk to.'

'He's very good, old Justin, really,' says Sidney thoughtfully. 'I'm a bit hard on him sometimes but I reckon that underneath he's a very capable bloke.'

'You'd reckon Hitler was a good bloke if he lit your fag for you,' I say. 'Come on, let's go and find a seat.'

We exchange a few cheery show-biz greetings with the likes of Glint, Dawn and Sandra and I settle myself down next to Mac. Samantha has told me how much she missed me while I was on location and there is little doubt in my mind that we will be indulging in a spot of festive in and out before the evening fades into the morrow.

This thought, coupled with the presence of Mac, reminds me of his filmic endeavours in the Cypriot knocking shop.

'Did you ever get any of that stuff processed?' I ask him.

'What stuff?'

'All that footage you were taking when Abdul ben

Knickers led the attack on that Greek town.'

'Oh, yes. Yes! I'd forgotten all about that. Bit rude some of it, eh?' He gives me a nudge in the ribs. 'I don't know what happened to that. It must have gone off to the labs with the other stuff because I put it in with the – Oh, Christ!'

'Hey! Where are you going?' I yell. 'You'll miss the start of the film.' It is most surprising but Mac has suddenly leapt to his feet and is pushing his way down the rows of seats towards the aisle.

'Don't worry about him,' says Sid. 'He's probably been taken short. I wouldn't say no to a leak myself. It's the excitement, I suppose. It's going to be very interesting seeing this for the first time, isn't it?'

'Yes,' I say, noticing that the Fight Unclean Culture people are sitting right behind us. 'Very interesting.'

The lights go down and Sid takes a deep breath. 'Here we go,' he says. 'Mac's going to miss it if he doesn't hurry – Blimey! That's unusual, isn't it?'

It is indeed. The picture on the screen is upside down.

'Gets your attention, I suppose,' says Sid. 'Cor! Love a duck, what's that?' It is indeed difficult to see what is happening on the screen because the picture is very fuzzy. Large objects seem to be revolving before the camera and we might be watching a close-up of pigs feeding from a trough.

'Thank gawd your father isn't here,' says Sid. 'He'd never understand that. I wish they'd get it in focus. Oh!!'

The gasp that goes up from the audience is like gas escaping from a punctured airship.

There, for the whole world to see is me, stark bollock naked with six naked birds clambering all over me. For a long second there is a close-up of my face telling Mac to piss off and then it is buried in an avalanche of flesh. The camera pans and – oh!! Oh no!! The audience's screams are cut in half by the shrill bleat of a police whistle.

'Stop the film!'

'Disgusting.'

The lights go on and strong arms drag me to my feet.

'Sidney Arthur Noggett and Timothy Makepeace Lea, I arrest you in the name –'

'It's all a mistake,' I squeal. 'They got the wrong film. I had no part in it.'

'– and anything you say may be taken down and used in evidence –'

'Oh my gawd,' says Sidney. 'You've really dropped us in it this time.'